Through These Eyes

Tales of magic realism and fantasy

By

Donna Maree Hanson

Copyright information

Through These Eyes first published by Donna Maree Hanson 2018

Copyright © Donna Maree Hanson 2018

National Library of Australia Cataloguing-in-Publication Entry

ISBN   978-0-6482795-6-3 (ebook)

ISBN   978-0-6482795-7-0 (Print on Demand)

Cover design by Patty Jansen
https://pattyjansen.com/store/

Proofread by Jason Nahrung

Table of Contents

Introduction 1

Through These Eyes I See 3

Compost Juice 17

She'll Be Right 38

Life Stealer 51

Veg Out 67

A Vagabond Rhyme 82

The Doctor's Pill 92

WWPRO 102

Verum Vivendi Sensus 116

Absence of Mind 123

In My Father's Footsteps 130

About Donna Maree Hanson 143

Also by Donna Maree Hanson 145

Introduction

This collection comprises some of my earliest published work and some more recent work, some of which has not been previously published. I have collected these stories here because they have common themes and feature elements of magic realism.

When I published my collection of science fiction short stories, *Beneath the Floating City*, I had planned this collection as well. With *Beneath the Floating City* being short-listed for an Aurealis Award for collected work, I feel excited to publish this collection.

Often my short stories appear to be about what is real and what is not real and how these can be hard to distinguish. For example, in 'Verum Vivendi Sensus', Beth sees people without faces. The question is, however, do people really have no faces or is there something wrong with her? What is the truth?

In some of my earlier stories I had a thing for 'bastard' products—items that are not what they seem. You will see this in 'WWPRO', 'Veg Out', and 'The Doctor's Pill'. I believe I was influenced by the great storyteller Roald Dahl when it came to the theme 'be careful what you wish for' in 'WWPRO'.

The stories 'Compost Juice' and 'In My Father's Footsteps' have not been previously published. Both of these stories have been hard to place and include elements of real life.

I managed to find a copy of my first published short story, 'Absence of Mind', and also 'Verum Vivendi Sensus', both of which had been electronically published back in 2001-02 and were no longer online or in my hard drive. I couldn't find 'Absence of Mind' anywhere, but finally had a clue as to where a copy might be. Thank god I did some backups all those years ago.

I owe a debt of thanks to Geoff Maloney for encouragement in those early days. He assisted in getting 'Absence of Mind' published with *Redsine* magazine through editor and author Trent Jamieson. I was very new to publishing at the time and I don't think I would have continued without that encouragement as I was writing novels, and short stories were where I was trying my hand at learning my craft.

In reading this collection, you might notice how my writing has progressed over the years. At least, I hope it has. I would like to thank the Canberra Speculative Fiction Guild for all their support from the beginning. From general meetings to short-story critiquing sessions, to publishing anthologies, the members work hard to share their love for speculative fiction and writing.

At the end of each story, I have put a personal note about where the story came from and other anecdotes.

Special thanks also goes to Ian McHugh, Kylie Seluka, Nicole Murphy, Cat Sparks, Russell B. Farr, Liz Grzyb and Keith Stevenson.

With thanks

Donna Maree Hanson
July 2018

Through These Eyes I See

Within these silvered walls, I see nothing but me in my skin. A multitude of sad eyes, crooked mouths, grimacing into infinity, with long clumps of tangled hair that writhe. Gazing at my reflection, I dream of being free—walking down the street and seeing the sky and hearing the laughter of the people around me. Then I remember what I would see through these eyes. It would overwhelm me, kill me perhaps.

The door swings open, a slight groan of the hinge. My breathing grows short and my heart beat thumps, squeezing the blood around inside me so fast I think that I will burst an artery. Now there is a gap in the mirrored walls where the doorway is.

'Mandy?' My mother talks quietly as she steps through the door. 'There is someone to see you. Someone who needs you.'

I see her reflected image, her wrinkled skin. By the cut of her mouth, I know she is determined. I whimper. I know they need me but it is so horrible seeing people without their skin. Sometimes they are rotting on the inside, great swathes of blackness eating through tissues and bones. I feel sick when I touch it with my gaze.

'It won't take a moment, baby. She is the same age as you but she is sick and only you can help her. Won't you help her? Won't you come out here and look?'

'Does she go to school?' I ask.

'Why, yes, she is in high school and very smart too. Before she got sick she won lots of academic prizes. They say she is a genius.'

'That means she is really smart, doesn't it?'

The reflected image of my mother smiles and nods. 'Yes, and you know smart people help the rest of the world, make it a better place. If you don't see her there might be some great discovery that never gets made, some new formula that never gets calculated...there are so many possibilities.'

'Can I see her in here?'

My mother frowns. 'In here?'

'Yes, that way I can look away when it gets too much and I can talk to her with her skin on, too.'

Her brow furrows over glittering eyes. 'Very well. But I don't like people seeing you in here. People will talk, think it's strange.'

In the mirror, I watch her turn and go, seeing her close the door with a snap. I watch my smile in the mirror. I've won a small victory. As it is not my healing day, she couldn't force me to heal or the government regulator would remove me from her care.

Soon after, the door opens again and a girl comes in. I like the look of her skin. She is slightly brown, a tan, I think it is called. She has bright green eyes and a wide, smiling mouth. Her dark hair is long and curled, bouncing around her shoulders. From looking at her skin you would not think she was sick at all.

'Hi,' she says, her eyes scanning the room full of mirrors. 'My name's Penny Woods. Wow, this is weird. Where do you sleep? Where do you pee?'

I point to the part of the wall where my bed is hidden and the cubicle where I wash and toilet. They are lined with mirrors too. There is also a television, which comes down from the ceiling, but I don't show her that. Most of the time, I control when I watch it, but when I am not cooperative my parents take the remote away.

She walks over, presses the stud in the wall that opens to my bedroom and bathroom, nodding while she turns her head left and right. Then she walks back. 'So you live in here all the time?'

'Yes.' I study her reflection as I answer her. I like the look of her skin. Trembling, I think about looking at her, looking through her skin. I wonder what rot infects her, what cancer is eating her, what defective organ she possesses.

'Do you have to touch me, hold my hand to heal?'

My hand shakes. I feel sick with trepidation. I hate talking about it, because the years of memories associated with seeing with these eyes come rushing out at me. It started with Aunty Lucy. I don't remember what triggered the change in me—some kind of blow to the head, some kind of trauma. I was three years old. I still remember the awful visage of her: skeleton grin, the fine sinews of her jaw creamy against the white of her jaw bone, bulging eyes and red, raw innards.

Great Aunt Lucy leaned in close to pinch my cheek, with her leering toothy jaw, and the soft flesh of her pink tongue sliding right back down her throat. I reached out and touched my forefinger to a lump that didn't belong right in the middle of her forehead. I could see through the bone into the gray mass of jelly inside. Later I learned I had touched the very spot of great Aunt Lucy's cancer and it had disappeared. People called it a miracle. Miracle. That word was often heard in my childhood, whispered and murmured around me, infiltrating my dreams.

'No,' I say to her reflection, after pushing the memories aside. 'I have to look at you, look at you without your skin.'

'Eww. That sounds disgusting. Go on then. Look. Tell me what you see.' She stands still and tall, her gaze on me, watching, calculating.

I suck in a breath and try to calm myself, try to steel myself to look away from the mirror and see her, see into her. I said I would look so I must do it.

I turn away from my reflection and raise my gaze. I start at the head, seeing into her, two perfectly formed hemispheres of grey matter, intricately folded, blood squirting through vessels, nerves singing with impulses. Nothing appears wrong there. Her bulging eyes orbit in her eye sockets, held there by sinew and muscle. The skull is perfectly formed. She has braces on her teeth, something I didn't see before. The breast tissue is growing still, and her lungs are clean and pure; so, too, are the chambers of her heart. Her lunch is digesting, tossing around in acid. She ate in a hurry. I see chunks of food not properly chewed. Lower I go and see nothing in the intestines, the uterus or vagina or bladder. My gaze travels down her legs, looking for tumors in the bone and the muscles. Everything is perfect. I lift my gaze again and do her arms. 'Turn around,' I ask her, wondering if I have missed something.

I take a long, slow look down her spine, look at her kidneys. There is nothing wrong with her. I frown and turn back to the mirror. My panting fills the room. She is looking at me with those big eyes of hers. 'Well,' she asks. 'What did you see?'

'Why are you here?'

She nods at me once, then paces the length of the room, her eyes assessing, her lips whispering, counting her steps. I did not think to check her mental state. All seemed so perfect inside her. She walks up behind me, hands on hips, her gaze meeting mine in the reflection.

'I came to see you. They talk about you—the urban legend—the great healer of our time. What did you see?'

I shake my head. 'Nothing. There's nothing wrong with you.'

She nods with a small smile, a look of satisfaction settling on her face, brightening her green eyes. 'Yes, there is nothing wrong with me.'

I feel anger. She made me look for nothing, for a game. If my guess is right, she paid my parents a lot of money to do that. 'I don't understand. Why did you make me look when you knew that already? Don't you understand how much I hate to look?'

I feel the tears, anger and hurt combined. I really don't get what is going on with this girl.

'I had to know if you were a fake.'

'A fake?'

She leans in close, her breath fanning my neck. 'Your parents have become very rich because of you. It could be a scam. Does it mean anything to you that they treat you like a freak, keep you prisoner?'

Her words cut through me. I see her with her perfect sight, her perfect body, her perfect health, and for the first time in my life I want someone else's life. Not mine...When I was a child my parents held me down as the people came near for me to heal them. I tried to run, to squirm, but they made me look and made me touch. Haunting images: muscles clinging to bones, ligaments pushing and pulling limbs, organs pumping and gurgling, cancers eating, diseases rotting.

My gaze focuses on her. 'Why? What is it to you?'

She walks across the floor, skirt swinging, legs smooth and long. She pauses and catches my eye in the mirror. 'I can't say. I'm going now. Don't tell your mother till I'm gone. I don't want—' she pauses '—questions.'

Again I see my eyebrows creasing into a frown. I do not like how it makes me look; it transforms me into someone sad, someone unsure. I hate being sad. I look up.

She is gone through the door, now swinging to a close. I'm alone again, looking at me in my skin.

Penny Woods has disturbed my equilibrium. In here I feel safe. I have never hated my parents for what they have done. It makes sense to me that I need them. They feed me, clothe me and let me have the mirrors. My parents took the money the people offered for my healing and they built me a bigger room—one with mirrors all around where I could feel safe in my skin. Without the mirrors, I would go mad. I have been in a room like this for as long as I remember. Memories of outside are so far back into babyhood, I don't recall the caress of the wind, or the feel of the sun, or even the sound of a bird.

My mother doesn't come again. My father brings me dinner on a tray, slides it along the floor without coming in. He never looks at me, or talks, unless it is necessary to tell me something. I crawl over to my food on my twisted legs, eat it mechanically, keeping my gaze on my mirrored self. I watch my expression as I chew and swallow, as I taste the sweet and the sour. I exaggerate the movements, making them larger and grander than they really are. I laugh at myself, at my vanity and my poor acting skills.

Another healing day comes. There are ten to do this time. I hate being outside of my room. I hate seeing with these eyes. I want to fight against my mother as she wheels me out to the healing room, but then I see a young child, spine twisted by a birth defect. I reach out and run my hand along the spine and feel it unbend and heal. The child whimpers and the mother cries out and then I am done and the child is whole. The mother's joy flows over me and I fight no more against the tide of those wanting to be healed and reach out to the next person. My mother never asks about Penny and, by the time I am through for the day, I can barely speak. Sedatives settle me down and I fall into a deep sleep. I hear noises in the night and feel my bed rocking. I hear a door slamming and voices but I can't wake; something is keeping me under the surface of consciousness. I drift away from the noises, feel my bed settle once again, thinking it all a dream.

I wake up. There is a different smell in the air. I wonder what it is. Had my mother burned the toast and not used the exhaust fan? I crawl out of bed and drag myself to the bathroom. Something is different and I wonder what it is. I think it is the light. It has a blue tinge, not a yellow one. I normally have warm yellow lights, not hard blue ones. I will have to mention it to my mother. Father must have put blue ones in by mistake. It is only a subtle difference. My eyes, though, are sensitive.

I crawl out into the mirrored room. The strange smell is here too, stronger. I inhale, trying to place it. 'Mother?' I call out. Normally, she can hear me through the monitor on the wall. I wait there, feeling slightly queasy and hungry. I do not like feeling this way. I dare not look at myself. I know there is nothing wrong with me. It is the sedatives and sleeping too long. I need my breakfast. I squint at the light around me. Here is it bluish, too, and its sharp edges hurt my eyes. A headache leaps up behind my eyes and I lean over, rubbing my forehead. The door swings open silently.

'Mother?' The tray slides in, gliding on the floor farther than normal. My mother doesn't answer. 'Father?'

The door shuts. No one speaks. Father doesn't normally talk so maybe my mother is out today. I look at my reflection. I talk to myself. 'You can talk to her later. She will fix the light, explain the smell.'

On my rear, I shuffle along the floor to the tray and inspect the food. There is a tub of strawberry yogurt. I pick it up and look at it. I'm allergic to strawberries. How could my parents forget? There is a boiled egg. I tap it open and yolk runs out. I nearly vomit. I eat hard-boiled eggs. There is Vegemite spread on my toast. I hate Vegemite. There is no peanut butter on the tray. I check the cup and it is full of dark liquid. I sniff, realizing it is instant coffee. 'This is not my breakfast. Mother! Mother!'

No one comes into the room. I am really hungry, but I can't bring myself to eat what is on the tray. Did I do something wrong? Are they punishing me? Have they gone on holidays and left a sitter who is an idiot?

I stare at the door. I will have to go out there and ask for food. I crawl over and then use the cool surface of the mirrors to help me stand. I curl my fingers around the rim of the door and pull. It doesn't budge. I'm not normally locked in. I choose to stay in this room. Why won't the door open? I slap it and call out more. Still no one comes.

Later, I push the tray by the door so it can be collected easily. I move from my usual position so I can see through the door when it opens. I want to know who is not looking after me properly. I press the stud in the wall for the television to descend. It doesn't come down. I try again and again, but no television. I am definitely being punished, but I don't know why.

The door opens but it is dark on the other side. I see the skeletal hands grasp the tray but nothing else. 'Wait please. Who are you? Where's my mother?'

There is no response. The door snicks shut. I feel helpless...angry. Turning to my reflection, I see the tension around my eyes and the grim turn of my mouth. No tears now. I wait for something to happen. I wait a long time until I wake from a doze. There is another tray there. I crawl over to it and inspect the contents. A dry meat pie, a glass of milk and an unripe banana. More food I can't eat.

I have been watching myself in the mirror for hours in the hard blue light. The door opens and someone steps through. My blood sugar is low now and I'm tired and sleepy. I turn to look at the person, seeing their ripe red muscle tissue pulling limbs. My gaze slides to the silvered mirror. It's her.

'Penny?'

Goosebumps break out on my skin. Seeing her there makes me feel very uneasy. My mother didn't announce her and I already know there is nothing wrong with her and so did she. 'Hi,' she says as her green gaze sweeps the room. 'Feeling okay?' she asks.

'I...you...what are you doing here?'

Penny flashes a smile. 'Just checking up on you.' She walks around the room, examining things like she did before. I feel very uneasy, like there are things inside me rolling around. I watch her, and come to a conclusion that seems ridiculous and true at the same time.

'Where am I?'

Penny turns back to me and walks up to the mirror where I huddle on my twisted limbs. I watch her with widening eyes as she approaches fast until her face is next to mine, right next to mine, breathing as I breathe.

'No point in hiding it. Though I do wonder how you knew. You are here in Mr. Sexton's house.'

'Who is he?'

Penny steps back, giving me space. She laughs and then her eyebrows arch. 'You don't know who he is? Why, he's a fucking legend: media tycoon, billionaire, computers...you name it, he has a hand in it.'

'Really...so what does he want with me...or you?'

Again Penny snickers, throwing her head back and running her hands through her hair, shaking it out like a beautiful wave. She is comfortable in her skin: I can tell. 'I work for him. He pays for my school, for anything I want. All I had to do was check you out, give him the specs for this...he wants to see you.'

'Me? Is he sick?'

Penny shrugs. 'Not that he says. I don't ask questions. I do what I'm told, get the money and then I'm gone. Before I head off you better tell me what you eat. He doesn't want you sickening.'

I give her a list of my foods. She doesn't write them down, only nods and smiles and then stands up. At the door, she glances a flash of green sparkling eyes over her shoulder before she closes it behind her. I shake a little after I am alone. I am scared now. This is not my home. My parents are not outside the door. I have no idea what this man wants with me. All I can do is look and heal. The door opens again and another tray slides in. After the door shuts, I crawl over and check it. I see that it is all okay and I stuff the food in my mouth. I chew and swallow, keeping my gaze on my reflection. The only thing that seems real and normal is seeing me in my skin.

It grows late. I don't bother to go to the bed. It's not my bed. I wash and use the toilet and lie down on the floor, my gaze on the mirror. I am asleep there when I hear a voice call to me.

Penny is there. 'Hi, Mandy. I've brought Mr. Sexton. You know, the good friend I was telling you about. Won't you meet him?'

I push myself up on my arms, try to shake the sleepiness from me and talk to her image. 'Okay.'

She reaches through the door and brings a man through by the hand.

'Mandy?' The voice is deep and gravelly, like it has spoken more than its fair share of words.

I start, blink a few times to see him standing there behind me. He's an older man, I think. Sort of like my father, but his hair is black and neatly combed. He wears a dark suit, and a thin moustache underlines a rather large hooked nose. The mouth is pursed, like he has been eating a lemon. I don't like the look of him. I'm not sure why but I don't like his skin. I look away but his reflection is in every mirror, multiplied to infinity. I have never seen that happen before. This room is not quite right, not quite like my home. I pant, and my palms sweat, and there does not seem to be any way I can escape his image. My eyes center in front of me, on the image immediately behind, on his face. His dark brows draw together when I don't speak.

'I want you to look at me.' His voice is a sharp cut.

He waves Penny away. She goes to the door, smiles at me once before leaving.

He tries to make his voice soft and coaxing, but it's no good. His voice sounds dead flat. His eyes are a no man's land: lifeless, endless holes. I close my eyes, shake my head. I don't even want to see him in his skin.

'Look. At. Me!'

My eyes snap open. I see him standing there, shoulders clenched, fists balled. I suck in a breath, my heart racing. What will he do if I don't look at him? Will he beat me? I have never been struck before, not since I was three years old. I've seen violence on television and I've seen people who have been beaten, cured them with my touch. I could heal the flesh but not the mental scars.

'Mandy. If you want to see your parents again you will look at me now. You will cure me.'

There is a weight to his words, like his throat has never laughed and joy is alien to it. I lift my eyes to study his reflection—the pallid cheeks, the slackness of the skin below the jaw, the dark menace of his eyes. His skin frightens me and I steel myself to look into him. Biting my lip, I turn. My vision lances through him and, at first, I am confused as revulsion fills me. I am vomiting up my meal before I even process what it is I see. It is corruption, rot, and death. The man before me, this legend of modern times, should be dead, yet he walks and talks.

I blubber and shake my head, pressing myself against the cool surface of the mirror to get away from the sight of him. My vision once again darts into him. I see how he is held together, bound by some unnatural force, a kind of sick energy that pulses within. Even his bones are yellow and brittle, as if they have been dug from a grave.

He stands there while I cry and writhe, fighting the awful image of him.

'You can fix it, can't you, Mandy?' His voice is as coaxing as chocolate on a turd.

I shake my head and cover the cry that escapes from my mouth with a trembling hand. 'No, I can't.'

'You will fix it. I will be whole again.' He turns and leaves me alone.

I collapse to the floor. My thoughts jitter and jump. I don't even know what he is. I don't know if I can cure him. I know I don't want to. 'I won't do it,' I say, and the words echo around me. I say it louder. No one comes to punish me.

The sound of the tray grating along the floor wakes me. I crawl over to it, but despite the yawning emptiness inside me, I cannot eat. Instead I crawl to the bathroom. In there the mirror shows my dark eyes and expression devoid of happiness. What little joy I had has been sucked out of me. In the night I dreamt of Mr. Sexton, my mind consumed by the puzzle of him.

My hunger rises after a while and I eat breakfast slowly, savoring the taste. A few hours later, Mr. Sexton returns. This time I am prepared and I am braver. He does not have to ask me, and he stands still as I climb to my feet and stagger in a slow circuit around him. I look through him from all sides, but I don't touch. I take the measure of him, and the spirit that drives him. I have the taste of him on my tongue. Through these eyes I see what I don't want to see. I nod and step back, slinking back to my position in front of the silvered wall.

'Well, aren't you going to cure me now?'

'Tomorrow,' I whisper. Without looking at him in his skin, I say, 'I need to prepare.' My gaze is turned inward. I am sorting through the images, the feelings and the awful composition of him. Parts of him are foreign: transplants, prostheses and black slime oozing slowly through hardened veins. He's not really alive. There is a force there, holding him together, congealing his innards, animating his flesh. It tries to hide from my sight but I can sense it and finally I see it poised there.

I try to sleep, to prepare for the next day. I think about the threat to my parents, but I think they are already dead. They would not have let me go willingly. They loved me in their way. I was their income and that has even greater value than kinship. That threat was not going to make me act. It was the consequences of my touch. Of what I would set free if I healed him.

Bleary eyed, I sit there to wait for him. He comes early as I knew he would. He scented that his cure was at hand. I see him in his skin. His flesh is even slacker now, grayish, it hangs loosely from his cheeks, and dark shadows rim those lightless eyes. I shiver in spite of myself, in spite of being very sure how to proceed.

I have no notion of how Mr. Sexton has come to be what he is. What deals he has made. What deeds he has committed. Whatever is inside of him is hungry. The corruption has a mind, the rot is eager for fodder and anxious to spread its influence. If I touch him I will set it free—free to roam, to conquer all. It could even come into me, take me...

'You will cure me now.' His face is locked down with determination. There is no room for feeling or inflection.

'I can't.' I try to avoid his gaze. The avid beast inside him sits behind his eyes.

'You lie.' The voice pricks holes in my skin.

I brush my gaze against his. 'I won't.'

A deep growl emanates from his chest. 'You will.' He is stiff with rage, hands clenched and rising to fists. 'I can make you. I can make your parents suffer. I can make you suffer...'

'I know...but...'

I nod, turn from the mirror and reach out. He stares at my hand and an eager glow springs to his eyes. I sense that force in him, ready to burst out. Yet he holds still, waiting for me to work the cure. Instead, I look down, look into my own skin. I ram my hand to my chest and stop my heart. The last thing I hear is his scream of outrage. The last thought I have is that I no longer have to see through these eyes.

This story came to first as a vision of the old aunty, leaning down to pinch the baby girl's cheek and the little girl screaming. A common enough occurrence. I imagined what the baby saw to give it such a fright. I imagined the face beneath the skin—the blood, the bone, the sinew. I then thought about the Medusa myth—but with the girl giving life, not taking it. I must admit a certain media mogul inspired Sexton.

Compost Juice

Next door, the Deagues pottered in the garden while I perched in the frangipani tree, singing 'London Bridge is falling down, falling down...' I didn't know all the words.

My two younger brothers played in the mud, slopping it and slapping it on each other. Mum and Dad were fighting in the kitchen. The back door was locked. That wasn't unusual—*outside and play you lot, children should be seen and not heard, silence is golden* and *shut the fuck up and get outside.* There were six of us.

'Don't hit Wayne with that garden fork, Doug!' I yelled from my perch. Before I could scramble down, Wayne had struck. I winced, but luckily there was no blood. After comforting Wayne, I pulled up a carrot from the garden bed, wiped some dirt off on my dress and handed it to him. Wayne chewed happily. Doug went to play with the hose and the forty-four gallon drum where we threw the snails we picked out of the garden.

At the wood paling fence, I tried to peer through the cracks. The Deagues interested me. They didn't fight with each other. They had no kids and were so ancient I thought I could hear their bones creak. There was this quiet to them, a slow, precise activity. I've heard Mum say many times that the grass is always greener on the other side. The Deagues had a very green lawn. Neat and trim, too, it was.

Flashes of color between the palings let me know someone was there. Pressing my face closer only gave me splinters on my nose so I snuck a quick look over my shoulder at Wayne and saw he was happily making mud pies and spooning them into his mouth with a stick. A look to the other side and I saw Doug had created a waterfall of snails as he overflowed the drum. All pretty good.

With one foot on the lower cross beam, I levered myself up. Hands gripping the top of the fence, I heaved enough to get my chin over. Mr. Deague noticed me straightway. 'Morning, Little Pearl.'

'I'm not Pearl. It's Jo. Don't you remember?' I giggled. He always called me Little Pearl.

He smiled and knelt down to trim the weeds under the fig tree. 'So what are your plans today, Miss Jo?' he asked while he snipped and snipped.

'The usual...hanging around.'

'Nice day for it,' he said as he lifted the brim of his hat and wiped his brow with his hanky. His hand trembled as he put it away.

I could feel the sun eating through my hair, gnawing on my scalp. 'How are the figs? Are you going to give us fig jam again this year?'

'I'm sure Mrs. Deague will make plenty to give to your mother.' There was a scream and a crash from our house. Mr. Deague looked up, eyes widening. I felt sick to my stomach. We paused, listening for what would happen next. There was another scream and the sound of the front door smashing closed. Both of us peered toward the road and saw Dad's old VW drive up the road. I couldn't see if Mum was inside.

'We love your fig jam,' I said, continuing the conversation. 'And the pickles. I love those with fresh bread and Kraft cheese.'

He frowned and then nodded. 'I make the pickles around here so I'm glad you like them, Little Pearl.'

'Are you finished, Mr. Deague?' Mrs. Deague asked. She had come along silently behind. Her wrinkled face peered out from under the brim of a large sun hat. She was peeling off her gardening gloves. The Deagues were so old they called each other Mr. and Mrs. all the time. Nana says that meant they were polite people, well-to-do or something. 'Hello there, Jo,' Mrs. Deague said with a smile, but there was something in her eyes, a weird kind of twinkle.

'Good morning, Mrs. Deague,' I said in the manner my nana taught me. Nana had a lot of time for the Deagues. They let her come over for tea. Not us, though.

Mr. Deague climbed slowly to his feet and brushed imaginary dirt from his knees. 'All done. I'll be in soon for lunch. I have to tend to the compost first. Miss Jo here was enquiring about the fig jam and the pickles.'

A smile added further creases to her wrinkled face. 'A few weeks more and then you will have your jam. No poking holes in the wax-paper covers this year, Jo.'

'Yes, Mrs. Deague.' I loved popping the covers with a finger and scooping out the top layer of fig jam. I got a hiding for it last year. Mum said it spoiled things. However, we usually ate all the jam and pickles within a month.

I climbed back off the fence as Mrs. Deague went inside their house and Mr. Deague went to the veggie garden—a sectioned off portion of their back yard up to the back neighbor's fence.

The sun was really powerful and I was hungry. I moved Wayne into the shade of the frangipani tree and told Doug to turn off the hose, while I went and banged on the back door. No answer. I peered through the little square of glass and listened intently. Mum didn't open the door. Had Dad taken her somewhere?

Wayne needed his bottle. I went to the front of the house. No windows were open there. I walked back down the long, steep drive and noticed that my window was open. I'd have to get the ladder and hope that Mum hadn't locked the baby in the room. It was quiet so Lisa wasn't awake yet.

Doug helped me bring the ladder up from the shed. 'Go and wait with Wayne by the back door. I'll open it soon.' Then I climbed up the ladder and crawled through the window. Lisa was sitting in the cot playing with some poo that had spilled from her nappy. 'Ew, Lisa. Stinky poo!' I checked the door and it was open. I ran down the hall to let the others in. I made a bottle for Wayne and gave Doug a cup of milk made from dried milk powder. I didn't want to clean Lisa up but she was crying now. I made a couple of peanut butter sandwiches for the boys and went to the bedroom. I noticed blood on the stair up to Mum's room. I chewed my lip and shivered a bit. I didn't know what was going on. Would Mum come back?

I put Lisa in the bath after peeling off her clothes and wiping as much poo off her as I could. I left her sitting in the bath while I put on the kettle to make her a bottle. Then I hauled her out, dressed her and put her in the highchair. The front door opened as we sat there eating sandwiches. We sat there quietly staring at the tabletop. Dad came in, thumping into the room with his big, booted feet.

'You eating?' he said like a grunt.

'Yes, Dad,' I said in a quiet voice. I wanted to ask after my mother but I got the feeling he was angry.

'Where's Lorrie and Stan?' I turned to face my dad. He didn't like it if you didn't look him in the eye when you spoke. He said he could tell then if you were lying.

'Um...Lorrie is with her friend, and I think Stan went out earlier.' I envied my older siblings as they were smart and escaped babysitting duty. Dad nodded and went to put on the frying pan. He made himself some bacon and eggs. I climbed out of my seat to make him some toast.

'Don't forget to bring in the eggs when you feed the chickens,' he said as he cracked another egg into the sizzling pan.

'Yes, Dad.'

I buttered the toast and slipped the slices onto his plate. 'Ah, Dad, where is Mum?'

Dad slipped his eggs on the slices of toast and tipped the bacon onto the plate. 'She's at the hospital. I'll pick her up later. She fell and hit her head.'

'Oh.'

'Yeah. I'll cook fried rice for dinner. Then you're all going to bed early, no arguments.'

I nodded. After taking the boys to their room, I put them down for a nap. I read a story from one of my library books. Doug didn't want to sleep and kicked me in the belly. 'I'll tell Dad you did that.' Doug just looked at me with his dark eyes, twinkling with hate. I didn't tell on him, but Doug stayed in his bed.

Lisa went back into her cot. I had to change the sheets first while she crawled along the floor and sucked on my slippers. I tossed some toys in there. Although it was hot outside, I went out to look for somewhere to lie in the shade. I didn't want to be in the house with him. With my dad.

The next weekend, there was no sign of Mr. Deague. The weeds began to grow under the fig tree, although the netting was there to stop the birds from attacking the fruit. I lay in wait for him, but still he didn't show. After playing in the stormwater drains all afternoon, I was heading home around dusk. (I wasn't meant to be playing in the drains, but I did.) I thought I saw movement through the paling fence so I leaped up, hoping to give Mr. Deague a fright. Sadly, he wasn't there. I looked around as best I could, perched with my elbows on the ridge of the fence. In the veggie garden, I saw Mrs. Deague carrying a parcel wrapped in white butchers' paper as she wove through the huge cabbage leaves and tall heads of broccoli. She dropped the parcel in the compost bin. I didn't call out. I just watched as she looked about, frowning at the garden. Suddenly she looked up and saw me. 'Miss Joanne Baker! What are you doing?'

With a twitch of her skirt, she hurried over to me. I could tell she was angry at me, but I didn't know why. 'How dare you spy on me!'

I leaned back, holding the ridge of the fence with my hands. 'I was looking for Mr. Deague.'

She paused, rearranged her frown for a minute. I couldn't quite make out her expression, but it turned back into a frown. 'He's not here.'

'Where is he?'

Her mouth turned down at the edges and the shadows cast by the dusk made her eyes into dark, empty holes. 'He's gone. He's gone to...to heaven.'

'Heaven?' I leaned my head one way and then another. 'Do you mean he is dead?'

'Yes, dear. He's passed on.'

I frowned then, from puzzlement. How had Mr. Deague died without me knowing? Why had no one talked about it? Mum had come home five days before. She hadn't said anything. Why wasn't Mrs. Deague crying? People cried when someone died. I looked at her clothes. She was wearing normal clothes, not black. Mrs. Osvaldo down the road wore black all the time. Nana said she was in mourning because someone died. A lot of the Italians and Greeks wore black. I guess a lot of them died.

'Off you go, you'll be late for your dinner.' Mrs. Deague turned away and walked into the house. I stared at her until she shut the screen door.

I climbed down the fence and ran inside. Mum was dishing up chicken noodle soup. The kids were at the table banging spoons and spilling snot onto their bibs. 'Mum, Mum! Guess what. Mr. Deague is dead. Did you know that he's dead?'

'What's dead?' Doug asked.

I went up to him and leaned in close to his face. His eyes went wide. 'It's when you don't breathe anymore or eat and it's like you're sleeping, except they put you in the ground and worms come and eat you and you turn to mush...'

'Shut up, Jo, and butter some bread.' Mum turned to cuff me across the ears. I ducked and she caught the top of my head. Doug started to punch Wayne, who started to cry, which set off Lisa in her highchair.

'Now look what you've started. I'll tell your father. You'll be sorry.'

I paused, my eyes widening. I fished out the margarine and buttered bread as fast as I could. When the noise died down a bit, I asked, 'So Mum, did you know? About Mr. Deague?'

'Hmpf?'

'Geez, Mum. He's dead. Didn't you know?'

'Yes, I saw it in the paper. I dropped a card off to Mrs. Deague. Now take these bowls over to the table. Be careful, they're hot.'

I did as I was told. When the soup was out, Mum went to lie down. My older sister came in.

'Is that all we have, soup?'

'He's dead.'

Lorrie sniffed at her soup and dunked a slice of bread in it. 'Not Dad?' Her eyes lit up.

'No, not him. Mr. Deague.'

'He was old. It was bound to happen soon.'

I concentrated on eating my soup and ensuring my siblings ate theirs. When my older brother came in, I jumped up from the table.

'Mum said you had to make the kids' bottles and put them to bed.' Before he could protest, I ran out of the room and hid in a corner of the lounge where I could watch the television undetected for a while. Dad hadn't come home. Lorrie said he was at the club. We made sure we were all in bed before he came home. That night I dreamed of Mr. Deague. He was snip, snipping, but instead of weeds it was worms. I screamed and sat up in bed.

'Shut up will you,' Lorrie said from the top bunk. 'I'm not taking you to the toilet.'

I huddled back down, afraid to sleep for a long while. I got a hiding in the morning because I'd wet the bed. Dad was pretty savage about it, rubbed my nose in it like Nana did.

A few weeks passed and no one talked about Mr. Deague. As far as I could tell, there was no funeral. It was as if he had never existed. I listened in on adults' conversation but no one talked of it. Another hot weekend came around. We were meant to weed the garden, but as soon as Dad went to the pub, we skived off. I went to find somewhere out of the way to sleep. Lorrie was stuck in the house, helping Mum with the kids. I grinned. No way was I going inside. I'd done my share.

As the sun lowered and the air cooled, I rolled out of the long grass where I had been sleeping in the shadow of the house. It was time to mix the chook feed and take it up to the chicken coop. I hated going in there. The chickens squawked, fluttered and tried to fly into my face. Their claws scratched and shredded my shins. When I put the bowl of feed down, they climbed over one another to get to it. Once they were no longer climbing on me, I went to collect the eggs, gathering them into the bowl I made with the hem of my shift. There were only eight eggs. The bantam chook hadn't laid an egg for an age. Dad was going to ask about it. He liked bantam eggs for some reason. Under the roosting boxes, I noticed some liquid, some black juice, and frowned. I squatted down and peered underneath and saw that it was oozing through the fence palings. It was coming from the Deagues' place. A waft of stench hit me suddenly, nearly making me drop the clutch of eggs resting in my skirt. It smelled like one of Lisa's nappies. One that had been left in the corner of the bedroom and maggots had nested in. Eww!

I backed away, locked the chooks in and took the eggs into the house. The next morning, Dad was shaking me awake. 'Get up, breakfast is ready.'

I looked out the window to the black sky. 'But it's night-time.'

'No it's not, it's 4.30 in the morning. I've cooked breakfast. Get up and help the others. I want you at the table in twenty minutes.'

Dazedly I rolled out of bed. 'Come on, Lorrie. We have to get up.'

I switched my nightie for a shift I found on the floor. Lisa was still sleeping so I left her in the cot. At the table, Dad placed a huge plate of bacon, eggs, baked beans and sausages. I gaped at my older brother. He looked scared. Lorrie looked cranky. Mum was there, sitting, saying nothing. Dad was banging pans and cooking up a storm.

None of us were eating. I wasn't hungry. I didn't know how I could eat all the food on my plate, but I knew I had to. Dad didn't tolerate waste. Many a time I had sat at the table for hours until I'd eaten the last of my peas. Dad dished out the last of the food and sat down. 'Eat up! Come on!'

We tucked in. I finished the last scrap of baked beans when the sun came up. I could hear Lisa crying and Doug and Wayne were screaming. I could hear them. They sounded like a fire engine's siren. 'Mum, shall I take Lisa her bottle?'

'Yes, and Lorrie, go fetch your brothers.'

Lorrie gave me a dark look. The brothers were difficult. Lisa just drank her bottle. Mum had already made it and the bottle was cooling off. I put my plate in the sink and charged up the hall to my room with the bottle in my hand. I'd just finished feeding Lisa when I heard some shouts. I peered out the door and down the hall. The noise was coming from outside.

Under the frangipani tree, I stood watching Dad and the rest of them around the chicken coop. I shuddered. *I shut it. I did shut it.* I could tell there was a problem. Doug had a little black chick in his hands. It was the only colored chick we had. It was dead. I wanted to run, but I stayed rooted to the spot.

Dad came past, a look of thunder on his forehead. 'What is it, Dad?'

He turned on me, walloped me one on the side of the head. I landed on the ground and blinked through the pain, my cheek burning. Dad was gone.

Mum was there, staring at me. 'They're dead.'

It was Stan who told me, when we were doing the dishes. 'All of them are dead. Mum says we won't get any more. Too much work and the local dogs get in and kill them.'

'But we didn't hear anything. How do you know it was dogs?'

'Mum said so.'

I placed a dinner plate on the table and grabbed another one. 'Was the gate locked?'

Stan nodded. 'Yes, I think so.'

'I'm going to see.'

'Not much to see. Most of the birds are gone, eaten all up. Nothing but feathers left.'

Through the fence I saw Mrs. Deague out and about in her garden. I didn't climb up and talk to her. I hadn't since she had told me about Mr. Deague. The chicken coop was carpeted with feathers. It looked like snow, like you saw in the department store at Christmas. There were no chickens. I checked the egg box but it was clean. I caught that whiff of stench. I squatted down and peered underneath. There was a black mark there, but it was no longer juicy. I stood up and scratched my head. I heard Dad calling my name and ducked down. I didn't want to get a hiding for something I hadn't done. As I squatted there, while Dad yelled for me, cursed me and then went away, I noticed that the fence was whole. There were no dig holes from dogs. No sign of the chicken wire being bent and shaped to make a hole. I stared at the gate. I knew I'd locked it but no one was going to believe me. I heard Dad's car drive off so I let out a breath and went back to the house.

Over the next few nights, my parents talked of weird pet deaths. Mr. Tucker over the back lost his two cats. He found only a tail of one of them. The Patricks lost two ducks and four chickens. They lived on the other side of the Deagues. I went snooping, by knocking on the neighbors' doors and asking to see the spot. In all I found the black stain and the horrible stench. Whatever was eating everything was coming from the Deagues' garden.

The fig jam and pickles arrived one afternoon the next week. I got back from school. Mum was in her room napping so I stole a look in the fridge. There they were, half a dozen tall jars of brown fig jam and half a dozen tall jars of yellow mustard pickles. I leaned in and popped a wax paper cover, digging my finger in and lifting out a fat piece of fig. I cast a look to the bench and saw that there was a loaf of fresh bread so I made myself a pickle sandwich, squeezed it so Mr. Deague's pickles oozed out, and licked it all off my hand.

That weekend, I was on the fence again. 'Hi, Mrs. Deague. Thanks for the jam and the pickles!'

She looked up with her wrinkled face and shook her head until her cheeks wobbled. 'Don't you get tired of climbing that fence? It's going to fall down, you are on it so much.'

I leaned back and looked at the fence. It looked pretty sturdy to me. I looked back at her. 'No. I like watching you from the fence.'

Mrs. Deague was picking flowers. She clipped them neatly and placed them in a flat basket. The Deagues had a very green patch of lawn. I wanted to play on it and feel the cool grass on my feet. The only way I could do that was when Mrs. Deague went to the shops. She turned her back to me and continued picking flowers. I turned in the direction of the Deagues' garden. The vegetables were very green and big. Cabbage leaves like elephant ears and pumpkins so big you could put a baby inside them. I compared them to our vegetable beds and ours looked sickly in comparison. 'How come your vegetables are so big, Mrs. Deague?'

She turned around and placed a white flower in her basket. 'It's the compost, dear. Mr. Deague looked after it.' She shook her head slowly. 'I suppose it's my job now. Once a week, he always put some blood and bone in it, straight from the butcher. Smells bad but the vegetables love it.' My mouth dropped open as I realized what she'd put in the compost. Just bones and some blood. 'Do run along, dear. I hear your mother calling you.'

I didn't hear anything at all, but I guessed she wanted me to leave her alone. It was getting hot anyway and my toes were getting splinters. 'Goodbye Mrs. Deague.'

I went to play with a tap in the shade, sloshing water all over myself and filling a bucket for Doug and Wayne. They were making ponds in the sand pit. Technically it wasn't a sand pit. Dad was forever chasing us out of it and smacking our bums when we spread the sand. It was for some work he had to do, but never seemed to do.

I kept an eye out for Mrs. Deague leaving for the shops. However, I missed her. Lorrie came in and said she'd seen her up the hill. I chewed my lip. I didn't know how long she would be getting her messages. Nana called them messages, but I never understood that. What messages did Mrs. Deague give the shopkeepers?

When I was sure she was gone, I snuck out the front of the house and climbed over the small fence to Mrs. Deague's yard. I did three cartwheels on their luscious patch of green lawn. I rolled in it and tumbled and then lay there smelling it and looking at a blade or two of grass, seeing the nicks the mower blade had made. I sat up and leaned on my hands, watching the vegetables. I wondered what the compost was.

In our house, it was where we threw the grass clippings. Dad didn't seem to do anything with the compost at all. It just sat there with white lilies growing around it. I remembered Mrs. Deague walking through the vegetable garden on a windy path with the parcel of butchers' paper in her hands. That must be the compost heap, I thought to myself.

Curiosity drew me on. I got up and headed toward the back. I checked the kitchen window, expecting to see Mr.

Deague, but he didn't peer out at me. I walked next to the large cabbages and saw there was broccoli, too. Tomatoes ripened on the vine and cucumbers also.

Once in the middle of the garden, I felt surrounded. It was like a jungle, a great place to hide and have an adventure. I sniffed and I smelt that awful stench I'd smelled the day before the chickens died. It was the same as the smell in the neighbors' places too. This was definitely where the black slime was coming from. It had to be compost juice.

Squatting down, I peered along the path. A black stain glistened in the sunlight. Farther on, I saw a box made with sheets of corrugated iron, painted black. It had a wooden lid. Mr. Deague must have made it. The neatness screamed Mr. Deague. I thought of him then and wished he was there to call me Little Pearl.

When I stood up again, I hit my head on a cabbage leaf. My breath *whooshed* out of me. I thought I saw the compost juice move. Breathing hard, I stared. I couldn't tell if the juice had moved or not. I tilted my head from side to side, trying to remember if it had been closer to the compost bin or me. I crouched down and walked closer. I covered my nose because I could barely breathe from the stink. Eyes peeled, I studied the compost juice. When it moved, I leaped into the air and screamed. One minute the black stain was just that—a stain—then it spread across the ground and under my feet.

The smell surrounded me, made me want to vomit. I was scared. I started to cry and hiccup. The slime stuck to the soles of my feet. I calmed down a bit, thinking *I'll just have to wash my feet*, when it moved again. This time it slid up my legs. Thick black ooze flowed up to my knees. Then it began to hurt. I screamed loud this time. 'Mum! Muuummmm!'

The black stain on my legs felt like burning, like it was eating into my skin. I was never going near any compost heap again. If only someone would rescue me, I thought furiously. 'Waaaa!' I cried like baby Lisa.

I heard something, saw movement. 'Jo? What on earth are you doing?' My head snapped around. It was Mrs. Deague.

Suddenly, the burning stopped. I looked down and the black stuff was gone from my leg. I gaped at the ground and the compost juice was gone, too. I searched for it and found it glistening next to the compost box.

'Jo!'

I ran to her, threw myself in her skirts. I was shaking. She patted my head. 'My, you are too curious and precocious, dear girl.'

'I just wanted to...to play on your nice green lawn and then...and then I wanted to...to see your compost.'

'My compost?' Her gaze narrowed. 'Whatever for?'

I lowered my head. 'You said Mr. Deague looked after it.'

'You are always spying on me. I don't like it.'

I gazed up at her and wiped some snot with the back of my hand. 'Spy? I don't spy. I like looking at you. You and Mr. Deague. You are so quiet and calm. I like that.'

Mrs. Deague let out a sigh. 'Very well, I will walk you home and talk to your mother. I have a special tonic for her.'

'What's tonic?' I was hoping it was something with chocolate on it.

'It's a special drink to give her strength. Help her feel better.'

ও∽ও∽ও

Mum started drinking the tonic that Mrs. Deague made her. Mum became energetic. 'Here you are,' Mum said when I got home from playing. 'I've baked some biscuits.'

She also cooked dinner, took us all to the park and did heaps of washing. I know because I passed her the pegs until we ran out. While we were in the yard, Mrs. Deague peered over the fence and said hello to us. I looked at her with her wide-brimmed hat and the hairs growing out of her chin and I figured Mrs. Deague was special—maybe a fairy godmother or a witch. She made my mother a tonic and it worked like a charm. She made a compost monster and smelly, yucky compost juice. I screwed up my face. Maybe Mr. Deague made the compost monster and now he was dead he couldn't look after it anymore. That meant it was Mrs. Deague's compost monster now.

After that, I often thought of ways to catch the compost juice. I thought I could use it on Dad. I took a jar and scoured the edge of the fence, where the chicken coop used to be. Mrs. Deague caught me at it, peering over the fence. 'What are you doing, Jo?'

I felt a bit shy about saying what it was for. I couldn't quite bring myself to convince my dad to go to Mrs. Deague's garden and get eaten by the compost monster. Not that I'd say it like that, but something like, 'Dad, have you seen the size of Mrs. Deague's cabbages? Her tomatoes are this big! You should go see.'

I stood up from where I'd been crawling along the fence. 'Mrs. Deague, do you think you could make a tonic for my dad?'

'Is he feeling poorly, dear?'

'No, I don't think so.' Just then there was a scream from the house—my mother's piercing shriek—a crash of crockery smashing on the floor and a dull thump.

I looked up at her, my eyes wide with pleading. 'It's just that...'

She gazed at the house, her expression kind of sad, her mouth growing into a grim line. 'I wish I had a tonic that could help your family, Little Pearl.'

My heart sank. I thought she could do it. I smiled at her, though, because she called me Little Pearl. 'Can you teach me stuff, Mrs. Deague?'

Her gaze snapped to me, her mouth a big 'o' of surprise. 'Stuff?'

'You know, how to make fig jam and...er...pickles.'

She nodded. 'How old are you, Jo?'

'I'm turning nine soon.'

'I suppose you could help out. I was going to make grape jelly on Saturday and that is almost as good as fig jam.'

I grinned. 'And can you teach me how to make compost?'

She gaped at me for a minute, then swallowed. 'Compost, Jo?'

'Yes, Mrs. Deague. Your special compost. I'd like to have some here to help my dad in the garden.'

She peered over the fence, her gaze sweeping our garden and taking in the overturned basket of dinky old clothes we used for dress-up and a bucket. Weeds hung over the sides of our garden beds. 'And what do I get in exchange for all this teaching, young lady?'

I chewed my lip and thought about it. 'I can help you in the garden. Weeding, snip, snipping?'

She nodded and smiled a little smile. 'Yes, that would be helpful, dear. I'm getting old now. I won't be here for long. What I would like most is that you didn't climb on the fence and peer over it anymore.'

My stomach dropped. 'Oh?'

'Yes, dear. If you want to talk to me or see me, come and knock on my door. I don't bite.'

She winked at me and wandered back to the house. A big smile grew on my face and I felt all warm inside. I was invited to the Deagues' house. I would wash my face and hands and put on a clean dress and then I'd sit on her sofa and have a drink of tea and fruit cake.

Wait till Lorrie heard about that. I climbed the fence one more time and stared at the garden, where the compost monster lived, and ignored the sounds of my parents in the house. I had something to look forward to. Mrs. Deague was going to teach me to make compost.

෴

Not long after my eleventh birthday, I was out in the yard, tending my compost heap. I'd snuck the leftover leg of lamb and dumped it in, hoping to lure Mrs. Deague's compost monster to my compost heap.

Only it wasn't her compost heap anymore. Mrs. Deague had died a few months before and new people lived there now. They didn't like the garden at all and now it was all weeds; the luscious vegetable patch, once filled with large-leaved greens, was now a wasteland.

There was no well-built house for my compost like Mr. Deague's, just a glorious pile of veggie scraps, grass clippings and bones. It smelled really bad and if you pushed around at the bottom, there was black compost juice underneath. I put the garden fork in and—*whoof*—a big cloud of stink hit me. I turned the compost over, happy to feel the juice splash on my toes. I'd stick them in Lorrie's face later and watch her squirm.

A shout reached me. 'Jo, get over here.'

It was Dad. His face was red like a tomato and his hands were curled into fists. I was sure I hadn't done anything wrong. I dropped the fork and raced down the garden beds toward the frangipani tree. 'Yes, Dad.'

'You forgot to pick up your brother today and your sister had to do it. You're always making Lorrie do your chores.'

I swallowed. 'I'm sorry, Dad. I forgot.'

It wasn't my job to pick up my brother, but I couldn't say that. Obviously, he'd been at Lorrie already.

The hand swiped at me, caught me hard. I fell to the ground. Before I could crawl away, Dad had me by the foot and was tugging me up. His hand fell on my backside and legs. I screamed. He held me hard, beat on me like I was a drum. I thought I would die. Fear and pain and me squirming and trying to breathe between my cries.

Then his movements changed. He stopped hitting me and his hand went into my undies, his finger probing inside the crack of my vagina. 'No,' I cried in mindless panic. I knew what he'd been doing to Lorrie since she got breasts. I didn't want him to do it to me. I kicked and, being upside down, caught him in the chin. When I landed, I scrambled away. I ran, ran to my compost heap.

He followed with a roar. 'Don't you run away from me. I haven't finished with you yet.'

With the tines of the garden fork, I held him at bay. We circled, him fierce-angry, and me huffing for breath. I hurt all over and tears made my vision blurry. I held the fork in one hand and wiped snot and tears from my face with the back of my other hand.

Dad raged at me. 'You're going to get a good hiding now, girl. I'm going to tie you to the bed so you can't get away. You won't get nothing for dinner. No one will come no matter how hard you cry.'

I shivered. He'd do it, too. I'd been locked in without food before. I never wanted to be tied up by him. The smell of drink wafted off him. He was too far gone to be reasonable.

He lunged and grabbed the fork. Before I could dodge, he had me by the hair and dragged me up against him. His fingers tweaked my tiny nipples and I screamed, surrendering myself to the oblivion of mindless fear.

The stench of the compost wafted over us. I closed my eyes, went limp. He tossed me to the ground and groped for his belt. I willed the compost monster to save me. I smelt the juice oozing out of the heap. I was too scared to look. The belt fell, slicing me across the thighs. I couldn't move as the pain paralyzed me. He'd used the buckle end. I thought I was going to die. He was going to kill me and there was no one to help me.

The second swipe didn't land. I heard a gurgle and cracked open my squished-up eyelids. Dad was like a shadow man. All black. Squinting, I saw clearer. The compost monster was on Dad's face. His arm had a twist of blackness on it.

Reverse crawling away, I gurgled in horror. The look on his face as he tried to scream made me bite my tongue as the black compost juice slid in, dove into his throat. He fell to his knees onto the compost heap, then keeled over face first, disappearing into the rotting vegetable matter. Muffled cries came from beneath the rotting bits of pumpkin and tea bags. A bunch of old leaves fluffed upward and settled down. The white lilies at the back swayed back and forth. Then it grew still.

My breathing still ragged, I looked around me. It was near dark. The new neighbors were out and we had nothing but the stormwater drain to the other side. No one would have seen what happened. I panted some more and cried hard. I was safe now. He wasn't going to harm me. I waited a bit longer, but Dad didn't come up. He didn't raise his red face to scream at me. He was gone. Taken by the compost monster.

Sobbing, I picked up the fork and piled more compost over where he'd been. It was time I got a hold of myself. I didn't want Mum asking why I was crying or have her clip me behind the ears to give me something to cry for. No, I was going to be calm.

The black juice came flowing out of the compost heap and a great waft of stench flowed over me. Keeping my feet out of it, I turned and limped back to the house.

No one would know where he'd gone. No one would be sad he'd left. Mrs. Deague had taught me well. She'd given me the tonic to help my family.

'What's for dinner, Mum?' I asked as I went inside.

This is probably the most autobiographical story I've written. Parts of this story come from my life—a hodgepodge of moments from my childhood. Some things never happened, of course. We did have these old neighbors and I did climb the fence and pester them. Unfortunately, there was no compost juice monster.

She'll Be Right

Above me, the wet ceiling sags. A steady drip pings and plops into a bucket. Outside, the rain sounds like applause as it smacks against the tin roof. Forget cats and dogs. You'd never hear them growling and mewling over that cacophony. Already the wind has picked up, grabbing the sides of the house, wrenching, whining and thump-thumping as the fibro cladding rips away. A deep groan trembles the floor boards. The house is coming loose from the pilings again. The flood levels must be rising. Nothing left to fix it. My home is on its way out.

A few storms ago, next door lost its corrugated iron roof and now the house slumps within its bent, twisted frame and naked trusses. All that remains of the inhabitants is a bone-ribbed dog. It's too far gone to bark and howl after two weeks on its own. Its master is never coming back. When I edge up to the window and wipe the grime from the glass, I can see it there, standing on shaky, skinny legs, shivering, its eyes dark holes in a bone-ridged face. I wonder if that's what my place is going to look like soon. Another loud scrape from under the floor, then an almighty quiver as the house yaws on its stumps. At this rate, my home will float away with me inside.

My stomach punches with hunger as I gaze out at the grey slur outside. No smoked roo left. Ate the last of it day before yesterday. I scoop up a handful of water to ease the pangs. It tastes musty, stale, and is slightly gritty. Brown ceiling fragments litter the base of the bucket and they stick in the grooves of my teeth. The plaster is probably poisonous—so much is in St Mary's. These old fibro bungalows were only meant to be temporary, but they lasted much longer. The munitions factories are gone, but these places, built for the workers, remain. For now.

My gaze sweeps the room. The end is near for this old place. I spit but the grains scrape the roof of my mouth, and I'm certain it's going to kill me. Too much past, too much transmutation during the war and after. The poison is in the very air.

Those munitions factories and nuclear dumping grounds seeped bad magic into the land. They weren't expecting the sea to rise and the ground to fall. Don't know when the rain started. It just rained and rained.

To search for food, I have to go out there, into that. Pushing my nose up to the window, I scan from right to left. No one is near the house, or down the alleyway. The gangs have gone, but there are desperate others who would venture out in this weather, particularly if they are as hungry as I am.

The brown stain of the road oozes past my back door. It passes beneath the house, the slow crawl eating away at the foundations. I wonder if my house will be here when I return. My tongue worries at the residue in my mouth. Maybe I don't want to come back. There's nothing here, except misery. I wipe my runny nose with the back of my hand then go inside to get my coracle. It's the only way to ferry myself to the murk.

She'll be right, they say. She'll be right.

No shes left in St Mary's. Haven't seen one since my mother left on that barge to cross the flooded Cumberland Plain. Some say the women drowned, some say they live on Dover Heights Island, and others say they went to the North Shore Plateau to escape the rot and the inundating seas. Don't know for sure. Just that they're gone.

The coracle is in the back bedroom. I built it from salvage—old plastic bottles, reeds and other flotsam. My cloak of plastic bags hangs limp as I plop the coracle out the back door. The rising water sucks at the base, making the bottles gurgle. The house growls out another protest and the floor moves beneath my feet. If the house goes I'll have no more ties to the place. Clenching my fist, I silently scold myself. That kind of attitude will kill me for certain.

I lean out from the stoop, foot on the coracle so it doesn't drift away. Harry, my back neighbor, retreats from his open door, trying to hide from me. *Nutter.* He's been dicey for a while, since his ceiling caved in and the possums attacked. The scars have mostly healed. At least he still has some of his fingers and a nose. I heard the screams and I could picture what was happening to old Harry. But it's every man for himself these days. She'll be right. Just look away. And what had he ever done for me? Nothing.

Over my shoulder, I glance through the dark mouth of my door, wondering what will tumble down from my ceiling when it finally collapses. What creatures live up there, nibbling on the plaster, the old insulation and electrical wiring? Something does, of course. Everyone has something in their ceiling. Something lives in the murk, too, but it's dark magic, bad magic. You couldn't defeat it even if you tried, so it was said.

With a broom handle, I push out from the back steps and let the current drag me into the sludge way. The old rail track embankment, always submerged these days, creates a current that directs the ooze toward the murk. I saw a map once that showed how the Penrith Lakes grew bigger, and the South Creek just down the road burst its banks and kept on coming. It spread over the whole area, eating suburb by suburb— Werrington, Ropes Crossing, Wilmot, St Mary's—and digging into the tunnels and bunkers of the munitions factories and the waste dumps, raking out the filth.

The road is thick and boggy and the coracle is like to run aground. A few good shoves and the resistance fades. I've skidded onto some new rain that creates a slick surface to glide over. At first, the passage is bouncy as I navigate past the rusted car bodies and remains of outbuildings.

Along Camira Street, the ruined houses stand naked from years of pounding rain and sucking winds, their doors empty mouths and windows dead eyes. Holed fibro walls intersperse the red-brick skeletons of a later era. Sheeting rain blurs their outlines, making them sway and ooze. The gangs caused the first damage, opening them up for the elements to do the rest. It was the gangs, their rampages, that drove the women away.

The memories make my body shudder. Mustn't remember that stuff now because once in the murk, those things can become real. Must think of good things, like food and warm fires and the smell of roo smoking and drying.

The current pulls me along, slowly but steadily. The intersection of roads is a bog, with a rippling surface of newly fallen rain. Using the broom handle, I beaver my way through. Fingers of mud climb up the sides of the coracle, grasping, tugging.

I pole harder, thumping at the surface of the mire to push me farther into the main drag. Here the road drains into the dark lake, choked with years of detritus. The ruins of a school rise up from the murk like the gates of hell. Beyond is the expanse of mud. There was a vast sports ground here once. People played games here. It's hard to picture. This is where the filth centers, where the evil lurking in the factory bunkers and the buried waste gravitated.

Soon it will merge with the rest of the flooded Cumberland Plain and then who knows what will happen.

Maybe it will just disappear, wash away entirely when it joins up with the drowned Parramatta River and the Sydney basin. I wish the sea would lick the murk clean but the evil filth is more likely to gulp the plains down whole, leaving nothing but a black stain. Perhaps it will turn West and learn to climb the Blue Mountains, or reach East to Port Jackson and eat the women hiding on the islands and plateaus of Sydney town.

Already I'm soaked through, but I pull my plastic cloak tighter. Greasy with rain, my hair lies in clumps, thrown into my mouth whenever I haul in a breath. Ahead, more coracles lurch along, converging on the main drainage route to the murk, the occupants' eyes peeled for roo floaters. If only it were that easy. I keep my distance. Every man for himself. She'll be right, mate.

Kangaroos paddle through the lake of grime, sometimes, endeavoring to reach the other side where the grass still grows on the higher ground up near the faded mountains. They try to swim it, finding no easy way around, and some of them fail. They come from the East, fleeing the wet that's devouring everything and burying it in black.

The coracles are bobbing. All of the occupants keep their distance from one another. A stab of thunder makes me start. The rumble continues, its deep bass echoing in my lungs. Men shouting. Three coracles together. I watch them, considering whether to go around rather than being drawn into any ruckus. People do not mingle. They do not work together. That grouping of coracles means trouble.

I draw the broom handle out of the sludge and listen, all my senses alert, waiting to hear whether the tones are hostile, the gestures angry. From this distance all looks calm. They appear to be converged on something of interest. As the current brings me closer, I see Geddy, who lives down the end of my street in the remains of an apartment building. Never outwardly friendly, he does barter items from time to time from his towered fortress.

He knuckles his forehead as he recognizes me, shifting the hood of his green plastic cape. The two other men I don't know by sight. They glare at me and then relax when Geddy says, 'She'll be right. Just Miko.'

They do not smile as I drift closer. They balance on their coracles with small knives poking out of their trouser pockets and their shoulders hunched, suspicious and ready.

'Miko, nice day,' Geddy calls.

I angle closer. 'Ho, Geddy. She'll be right?' My coracle bounces against his. He uses his foot to steady me.

Geddy nods. 'Nothin' much. Best move along now. Every man for himself.'

A tentacle of some kind floats beyond the gathered men. A grey, lifeless lump of meat. I scrunch up my nose. 'Edible?'

'Dunno. That's what we're discussing. Never seen anything like it. Thought maybe it was a bad omen. Being so odd now.'

Fear ripples inside me. I nod. Maybe they will fight for it. I want none of that. 'I'll be off then. Every man for himself.'

Geddy nods again. Anxiety clouds his features. I pole away and I do not look back. I try to push that tentacle from my mind, because if I don't, I might try to imagine what type of creature it came from. Better off to think of chewing on dried roo. Dried and smoked. My mouth waters then and my stomach punches and pounds. *Feed me, feed me.*

Dried, drowned kangaroo is not great, but I've had years to get used to it, when the tinned food ran out. The vegetable patches died from rising salt and damp. I pole harder, eager to catch me some dead kangaroo. That tentacle pops back into my head. A mutated maggot? The thought almost makes me barf. *No! Mustn't think of it. Must forget I ever saw it. Move along. Nothing to see or think here.*

I glance back at the three men, hearing their words over the swell of water and the rain spattering the surface. Their junk-made coracles bob in the choppy current.

'Looks like something chewed it,' says one of them, his shrill voice cutting through the background noise.

A prickling sensation begins on the back of my neck, all hot and dire. Mustn't think about what chewed it.

Poling on, the stench grows overpowering. It infiltrates my nostrils, crawling inside of me, twisting its poison into my gut. I gag once or twice and then concentrate and breathe through my mouth. I know where I'm heading. The best dying place, where the roos, exhausted from their swim, fur tangled with mud, flounder and drown only meters short of their goal.

The memory of the floating tentacle keeps coming back. I search the surface of the sludge for strange folds that might predict the emergence of a slime monster. *No. No. Must think of something else.*

She'll be right. Every man for himself. That's what they say. That's why the women left. They'd had enough of it. The blind witnesses. The deaf witnesses. The witnesses who couldn't be bothered to help anyone. No brotherhood of man. Just every man for himself. We'd like to blame the murk for this bad magic yet it existed long before the murk. We have the bad magic inside us. I know that. I see it every day. Even the pages of the faded and drowned books talk of it.

Looking back over my shoulder, a sense of unease crawls up my shoulder, even though there's nothing to see.

The rain thickens, mixed with blown-up mist to make a paste that obscures Geddy and the others. That tentacle has me spooked.

If I hear a scream or two, it must be my imagination. Had their minds conjured up a beast from the deep? No, they are dragging the tentacle up, working together to salvage the meat. And tonight they will sit around a stove, drinking rainwater and watching its fat sizzle and spit, talking and laughing. Not bloody likely. But that's a much better image to hold than what my mind keeps conjuring.

The rain is so heavy now it fills my tiny vessel. I place my patchy cloak along the edges, hoping to keep the water from swamping it. My cloak's heavy edges drag into the sludge. I imagine things down there, reaching up to drag me under. A giant platypus with huge taloned feet, ready to puncture me and drag my poisoned carcass to the deep, where the sun couldn't reach, even if it chose to shine.

Movement up ahead. A disturbance in the surface of slime. My nightmare imaginings dissipate. A mob of roos has entered the murk, heading across.

Light brown froth marks their passage. They dogpaddle through the mud, using their hind legs and keeping their heads out of the water. Not made for swimming, but somehow they manage. No one and no thing would choose to swim here, unless driven by desperation or they were oblivious to the threat of bad magic.

I use my pole to angle me into the current, steering clear of the confluence of sludge ways. Sloping eddies of rippling, stinking mud, spreading its influence through once inhabited streets. The murk is growing stronger, growing fatter. Sucking the life from everything. A barren, blackened tree stump sticks up, next to it a rusting, four-pronged contraption once used to hang clothes.

I'm away from the edge now, zeroing in. Taking my gaze from the mob, I navigate through hidden obstacles— shed skeletons, floating planks of wood, clawed fingers of dead trees, all lurking there to snare the unsuspecting.

The rain increases, grey and close, reducing visibility. It hammers down so hard my ears hurt. No one is crazy enough to venture so close to the center. I want to catch the mob before it reaches the other side. Caution dictates I skirt along the edges, navigating around half-eaten houses, rather than kicking out into the middle, where it is the deepest and the vilest.

My stomach rumbles. Despite my hunger, I will need to dress the meat and smoke it so it lasts. First, though, I will eat a rare filet, suck it down my gullet and quell that beast.

Large, grey clouds convulse above, forking the sky with lightning. The clap of thunder shakes me to the toes. Fear quivers through my gut. I don't know what to do. I must go forward. Going back means starvation. Chewing my lip, I stay on target. A swirl of converging mud and water sluices me along, nearly tipping me from the coracle. Blinking hard, I use my forearm to wipe my eyes, my attention on the roo mob up ahead.

Surely, surely, one would tire soon. The murk is choppy, alive and angry. The roos are battling hard. Twenty-two of them in all. I keep them in sight so I can pounce when one fails to surface.

A trail of froth generated from mighty dogpaddling hind legs spreads out like a vee. I keep my distance, following behind. At this stage, the whole mob looks hearty and determined. Not a straggler in sight. Focused. I do not usually follow them this way. Normally, I'd skulk around the banks in search of floating corpses. Today I am drawn into their struggle. I squint to the horizon, trying to see their goal. Nothing but a grey haze up ahead.

How can they know that there is something more beyond the edge of the murk? Can they smell solid ground, can they sniff out sunshine? Is there some innate sense within them that can scent grass, or inhale hope?

On and on, they churn the liquid filth beneath them, heedless of obstacles and lurking death. I am losing myself in their battle for survival. One or two of them must die so I might live. Yet looking at them, making their way with energy and life, I find myself urging them on.

They stick together, that mob. Changing places, the back ones working their way forward, taking the places of those in front. The front ones dropping back to take a break.

I shake my head. Surely I'm dreaming—so hungry I'm imagining things. Mustn't think. Mustn't remember the tentacle, or the giant maggot, or the mutated platypus.

Maybe the murk is playing with my mind. The roos continue changing places while I follow them. Could they be helping each other, working together so all of them make it through?

I keep following. Bastards. That is what they're doing. Slowing down to wait for the laggers, assisting one another. No 'She'll be right, mate', here. No 'Every roo for himself'. These buggers are working as a team. Teamwork—by god, is that what that word meant?

I follow as closely as I dare. Maybe I will have to club one with my broom handle. The edge of the murk is visible now. I move in, but the mob speeds up as if they know I'm coming in for the kill.

The rain stops suddenly. Visibility clears. Fields emerge on the far side of the murk. Distant hills revealed in a sudden burst of sunlight. I blink and lick my lips. It's not often one gets to see blue sky. I find myself smiling, then when I see the first of the mob climbing out of the murk, my smile dies. Their fur is now black with gunk and debris: sticks, bits of old plastic, clumps of unrecognizable matter. As the other roos emerge, the first ones roll on the ground, wiping the detritus from their hides. I don't blame them. I wouldn't lick that shit off me either.

I balance in my coracle and gape. Not one of the roos failed to reach the other side. They helped each other and I'm alone and empty-handed.

I wonder at the view, the mountains beyond. Would there be food in that distant place? Should I follow, maybe kill a roo on the way? I think of the tentacle, floating sickly grey and lifeless. I catalogue what I could barter with Geddy for a piece of it. Nothing he didn't already have.

Balancing on the coracle, I stare at the roos, shuddering as one looks back at me. There's something in those eyes—intelligence. Is that a slight nod of the head? It's got to be my imagination. The roos bound off and fade into the distance, while my mouth still gapes.

The murk moves suddenly beneath me, causing me to lurch sharply to the left, and I fall out of the coracle. Blackness overwhelms me and the filth crawls into my lungs.

Breaking the surface, I struggle up, spit and hack the crap out of me. My coracle is upside down and sinking slowly. No hope of recovery. I tread liquid filth and twist my body around, trying to see what toppled me. Nothing, but the edge of the murk is close, no more than thirty meters. I can make it if I try.

Suddenly, the swell up thrusts, pushing me up and away from my sinking boat. Looking behind me, a scream dies in my throat. I will myself to unsee what I have seen. Wiping grime from my eyes, I see the monster is gone. Was it ever there?

I must get out before my thoughts make things real. With arms of lead, I crawl through the murk, tasting rotting meat and unwashed bodies. It smells like a blocked sewer, with turds swirling out of it; like mounds of shit with an overlay of vomit. And even then, there is something more, the taint of dark, bad magic. An ancient putrescence that is slightly sweet and musty.

I am going to die. Unless…unless I can make it to the bank. Unless I can crawl free of the murk before it consumes me. I'm sure I can. Give it a go. No harm done for trying, old man. I want to see the sun and the mountains. The rain has stopped. A patch of blue ahead, a shaft of sunlight. That's something I'd like to feel. Sunlight on my skin.

I lift my arm and arrow it down to pierce the congealed surface and drag myself forward while kicking for all I'm worth. I recall the roos bounding off, their tails propelling them forward, sticking together as they head for the mountains. I can do it. I can.

Using a handful of reeds, I inch my sodden body out of the murk, panting and sobbing, because the fear is still inside me.

When I catch my breath, my heart rate slows. The remains of St Mary's and its neighboring suburbs lie before me, pitiful and small against the lake of black that oozes around and between.

And here's me, on the wrong side of the lake and with my coracle sunk. But why would I go back, anyway? There is nothing for me there. No point at all. My home is crumbling, like memories of the past. I twist to look over my shoulder. Away in the distance, the Blue Mountains beckon, with clearing clouds and bright blue sky above.

I look down at myself, covered in black shit, twigs and plastic tendrils. The roos had this part right, too. I drop to the ground and roll in the grass until the murk comes off.

I stand there, stinking and gazing at the horizon, then back to where the roos had bounded away.

I turn that way.

If I want to live, I have to leave. There's solid ground somewhere ahead and mountains in the distance. Maybe I'll find some food on the way. Maybe I'll find something else. Limping, I jog after the roo mob, thinking, she'll be right.

She'll be right, mate. She'll be right.

The idea for this story arose out of a challenge. I emailed my partner, Matthew, also a writer, and said, 'I dare you to write a story'. And sent him the bucket scene. We were both interested in submitting for an anthology. He didn't go on to write anything, but I did, and the rest evolved from that initial challenge. It didn't make it into the anthology. Over the years, the story has been helped along the way by Kaaron Warren, Cat Sparks and Ian McHugh. I used to visit my grandmother in St Mary's. She had moved there in the latter part of her life. My mother had told me a bit about the history of the place and how my grandmother lived in an old workers cottages that had been erected to house the workers in the munitions factories during the Second World War.

Life Stealer

A cool breeze stroked Jake's neck as he gazed out over the Queanbeyan River from the veranda. He didn't mind the crispness in the air as it was a welcome reprieve from a series of long, hot nights.

The morning quiet cocooned him as he took in the bush-clad hills looming over the near-stagnant river and the housing estate surrounding it. Very soon the sounds of insects, birdcall and the yipping and barking of dogs intruded. Even with that background noise, he still felt it was quiet, so quiet and calm.

The scenery changed every day and yet it was so easy to take it for granted, to get up for work each day and not see it, not see the surrounding beauty. He remembered that from his childhood, living with a family that never understood his need to be close to growing things. Lucky for him, there had been a school teacher that took an interest in him and put him on a path to the ideal job—a park ranger. You'd think looking out over the forest canopy on bushfire watch would have cured him of looking at trees. Yet the canopy was always changing too, shifting color and shape, just as a tree was different from the next one, in its posture, its texture and its character.

Jake laughed aloud, picturing a copse of cranky trees. My, he was fanciful this morning, he thought to himself.

The screen door opened and Rick leaned out, hair on end, eyes puffy with sleep. 'You're up early, man. You goin' to work?'

It wasn't quite bushfire season, so no lookout for him today. It was time to plough through the papers on his desk.

'Soon. Just enjoying the view.'

'At seven thirty in the morning? Right. See ya later, mate.' The door clanged shut. Jake sighed. His housemates didn't quite get him. The house appealed because of the view of the river and the bush.

He dashed inside and put on his work shirt, hooked his phone to his belt, and stuffed his bag with his gear. Back out on the veranda, the sun brightened suddenly. He paused there on the stoop, looking out at the light as it played over the hills, seeing the dark clefts nestled between them, making him think of the secret shadow between a pair of breasts. The shadows moved quickly, dodging from one spot to the next. Some contracted and others darted to safe spots in a gully or under a rocky outcrop. Looking up, he saw scudding clouds, a large, slow one casting a sizable dark smudge beneath it. The shadows kept moving. His eyes danced as he followed them, liking how the light changed the colors, until he felt it.

One shadow was not like the rest. Jake closed his eyes and felt it there like a hard dark nut of something. There was something similar inside him: anger, resentment, a feeling of being lost. This dark spot was not his feelings. It was separate, alive, hungry.

Jake sent a text to the office to let them know where he was, then he secured his pack to his lower back and took off down the road to the riverbank. He had to get closer, had to see for himself. Cars exiting driveways filled up the roads. The place was waking up around him. He dodged a few cars and continued down the road. The ridge of hills rose up over him as he neared the river.

After climbing over the fence rail, he stood there, taking in the mallards waddling in the long grass as he contemplated the hill in front of him. Shifting his gaze left and right, he searched for that dark spot. Morning sunlight glittered oily on the surface of the sluggish water. The houses ran up close to the edge of the river in places. People talking, doors slamming and engines idling reached him. He had lost it. Temporarily frustrated, he lowered himself to the ground, rethinking its position in relation to home, while he ripped off the tops of the long grass, pulled them apart, shredded them, inhaling the sweet smell.

Alone with his thoughts, he could reach out to the world around him with his spirit. Since puberty, something had been growing in him. An awareness that was fleeting and powerful. It mainly came to him near the water or the bush. He could spot wombats on the riverbank before others. Find lost things in the bush, whether it was a handbag or a lost shoe.

The sunlight brightened as the clouds shifted again. The green of the grass and the darker green of the trees faded in the harsh light. Day was here, washing away the sticky cobwebs of night and revealing everything. He would have to move up the bank farther to locate that spot of darkness, that kernel of menace, he had sensed earlier. It was there, he was sure, just not visible from where he was. He could taste its pain, as if sunlight hurt it.

A rudimentary weir situated down the banks of the slow-moving river allowed for an easy crossing. Many locals walked their dogs or jogged there. The tracks cut into the bush—rough, faded pink clay paths held together by grasping tree roots. Dry, they were easy to walk along. He took a left and headed up the hill to the cleft where he felt the shadow lay.

The trees rustled around him as he climbed the path. Here and there, shafts of yellow sunlight filtered through the branches. A magpie flapped away. A couple of doves coo-cooed as they launched from a branch. A trio of roos bounded away at his approach. He liked the feel of the bush around him, the life, the energy. He threw his concentration forward to the place where the dark spot of hunger dwelled.

It was as if the darkness was drawing him in, stuck like a pin in the map of his mind. The track was well worn. Water had washed the clay, leaving gouges and revealing large stones and thick tree roots. His toes gripped the soil as he pushed his way up the hill, dodging low-lying branches and bushes. He angled right and up, following a twist in the track.

Sun-filtered spots hit the leaves and the scent of eucalyptus eased into the air as the day heated up. He drew near the spot, the base of one of the small hills, where the land rose up again, making a cleft where the sun rarely shone.

At his feet, he saw small dead things: dried corpses of possums, the dried hide of a wombat and the rotting frame of a young joey. He kneeled down and touched the ground, sweeping the dirt with his fingers. Tiny skeletons littered the soil: desiccated bodies of ants, millipedes, red back and huntsman spiders. Lifting his head to take in his surroundings, he saw that it was a dead space—nothing remained alive in that spot. At the base of the bushes along the path, he could see tiny white bones of ribcages, some with feathers clinging to patches of dried skin. Even the foliage on the trees and scrub was dry, dead and brown.

Voices on the ridge above him filtered down to where he crouched. He squatted down and ran his hands over the dirt. He wanted to feel what that thing felt. It was a live thing, he was sure—a spot of dead that had a mind, a will and a hunger.

A sliver of fear entered his mind. Could he trust this knowing he had or was he losing his mind? They said his mother was so crazy she hadn't been able to look after him, which was why he had ended up in foster care as a child. The memory of her was dim, faded. There was a saying, that insanity runs in the blood.

Shaking off the doubt, Jake closed his eyes and inhaled, sending his other senses around him. A leaf jostled by the light breeze. A blow fly landing on the wombat carcass and laying eggs. Already maggots were squirming in the dead flesh; there wasn't much left for the newly hatched ones to eat. He pictured the peeling bark on the gum tree behind him and the slow ooze of sap hardening on one side and the trail of dried, dead ants stuck to its trunk.

Below him, he sensed the carcasses of the dead earthworms, silverfish and cockroaches, and even the death of the deep roots of more-distant trees. The soil was dying. The trees here would die too, eventually. They were starved of life. The whole area had had the life sucked out of it.

The thing must have been trapped for a while, considering how deeply the death went and how wide. It was gone now. Left this spot. Took its chance when the cloud blocked the sun and shifted in the shade. He wondered where it had gone.

From the ridge above him, the voices came again, suddenly clear. He could detect fear in their voices. Something was wrong. Taking an upward path, he walked under shafts of light to where he thought the voices came from.

A smell of stale smoke teased his nostrils. It wasn't good that they had had a fire away from the approved camping grounds. He wondered if he should call it in. He frowned as he entered the small clearing where a small campsite had been set up.

A group of people huddled there and he saw that they were indigenous folk. They didn't start with surprise when they saw him but they stopped talking. It was an old woman with white hair and large sagging breasts who came toward him. Her eyes rested briefly on his uniform and name tag. Trailing behind her were two young men, probably twenty or so, and a snot-nosed kid about seven years old. One of the young men, shorter than the other with a scar on his chest, nodded and said, 'Bro...'

Jake nodded back but didn't speak. He found it hard to speak to indigenous people. The old woman moved toward him with an uneven gait, her dark eyes under white brows staring at him. She nodded as she moved closer.

'Who are your people?' she asked Jake.

'I don't know,' he answered. Could they tell his blood? Did they know if he was kin? Just then he realized why he felt uncomfortable. He was not part of them, didn't know them, their ways, their language. His father had been stolen from his family out bush somewhere and he had been too gone with drink to tell Jake what he needed to know. It was so long ago now and it didn't matter anymore.

'Why don't you know?' she asked him, still nodding as she sized him up.

Jake shrugged. He hated answering that question.

'I'm Pat. My people are the Ngunnawal people.'

The taller man came forward and offered his hand. Jake took it, surprised at the acceptance. 'I'm Birdie and that's Arlo, my cous, and that's little Bess.'

Jake nodded. Pat stared at him. He coughed to cover his embarrassment and stood behind his role as park ranger. 'I'm sorry, you shouldn't have a fire here, shouldn't camp here either. If you have a map I can show you where the designated camps are...'

The old lady nodded but she wasn't listening. Her gaze moved to the bush around them, searching, waiting, hoping. On top of the hill, they stood together while she sniffed the air and then her gaze returned to him.

'Is there something wrong?' he asked her.

Her eyes lowered. 'We're looking for someone.'

Jake lifted his chin. 'I'm looking for something.'

Her left eyebrow lifted and the taller boy moved forward and whispered to her. She nodded as he poured words into her ears.

'What do you know?' she asked him again, her gaze now travelling over him and behind him as if he had brought more people with him.

Jake hunched his shoulders, feeling uncomfortable with her scrutiny. They were all looking at him, even the snot-nosed kid. He didn't want to talk about the feeling. He didn't want to hear their laughter and their scorn.

Then the little kid, Bess, said, 'Please."

Jake struggled, trying to frame the words, logically and well-reasoned, and then realized that he couldn't. Not like that. He'd have to speak from his heart, from his true self.

'I felt something, something hungry, something that leaves bones behind.'

The old woman nodded. None of them was laughing.

'Who are you looking for?' Jake asked her.

'My grandson, Lee. Went missing during the night. I think he strayed from his bed. We were camped, just for the weekend. We live in Canberra but we like to come here and be on the land sometimes.'

'He's lost in the bush? You check the river?' Jake asked.

'Yeah. We did,' said Arlo.

'Aunty, why are you wasting time talking to him? We should go looking again,' Birdie added.

Pat kept her eyes on Jake, assessing, measuring. 'He knows somethin',' she said at last.

Jake stepped back as the two young men, bristled, gathering their muscles, transforming from friendly to aggressive with a breath. 'Tell us.'

Pat shook her head. 'Not about Lee, about what is out there, what might be dangerous to him. How to track it...'

'I'll call in the police,' Jake said.

'Wait,' she said. 'You can help us.'

Jake was not sure what to do. Then he felt it, felt the presence shifting around him, away then closer. Above, stray clouds cast running shadows. The thing was moving again. Jake wished he was a bird so he could look down, pinpoint it in the trees, in the shadows. He had a stray thought that if he stayed in the sun he'd be safe. But safe was not on his mind. He wanted to help find the little boy, keep him from the thing.

A shiver passed through him. It wasn't something, some oddity; it was a threat to him, to the missing kid. 'I should get help.'

'If you don't find him, then call for help, but later. Go now. I have a feeling there is not much time.'

He nodded. His phone had a satellite connection. He could call it in. 'Do you men have a light, a torch or something?'

Birdie nodded and went to the pile of belongings and brought over a couple of torches, checking that they worked as he did so.

Jake undid his pack and drew out his own. 'Keep them with you.'

Birdie wrinkled his brow. 'But it's daylight and fully sunny. What do I want a torch for?'

'The search may take a while, until night even. Or you may go into a canyon, into shadow, and then you'll need it.'

In the dirt, Jake drew a rough map of their position. 'Birdie, you go into that section, search closely, look for anything. Arlo, do the same thing but here. Do you know the rocky outcrop? Good. We'll meet there in three hours or so. I'll take this section.'

The young men nodded. 'What about aunty?' asked Birdie.

Jake had seen how difficult the old woman found it to walk and knew she couldn't go down the ridge face.

Pat picked up on his hesitation. 'I'll keep calling out to him so he knows where we are. Go,' she said. 'Follow your feeling. Keep looking."

Jake darted into the scrub, trying to escape the rocking emotions the encounter had caused. Meeting them had opened up a part of him he thought he had put away forever. He breathed slow and deep, trying to immerse himself in the bush once more. He needed to stay focused because a child was in danger.

Pat yelled instructions to her nephews. They made noises as they pushed into the bush—clump, clumping and snapping branches. The sounds put Jake's teeth on edge. Jake glided through the bush, carefully shifting branches and passing over fallen ones without snapping them. Not far in, he found signs of the boy's passing. There was a sock, dirty and covered in dried leaves and small twigs. There was also a broken branch, low down, like where a child would be.

There was a smell, familiar and rank. Death. Old death. He widened his search and then centered on the spot from where the stench emanated. He drew nearer, his heart beating hard in his chest. He saw the khaki walking boot first. At an angle, the naked ankle bones protruded. The corpse was dried and shriveled. A lost bushwalker maybe. The clothes were fairly clean and dry and there was a backpack nearby, covered in leaf fall.

Jake pulled out his phone and dialed the office. 'Yeah, it's me, Jake. Look, I'm out here at the ridge out the back of the Queanbeyan River.'

'Aren't you on duty?' the receptionist asked.

'Yes, kind of. Look, I have a situation out here. I need to report a body. I'm going to message you the coordinates. I'm searching for a lost kid right now, but let the cops know and I'll guide them in. Okay?'

The receptionist rang off, promising to let all those who needed to know what was going on. Jake checked the coordinates on his GPS and then texted them to the office. Jake finished up examining the site and then moved on.

Signs of small deaths, of the little lives stolen—baby possums, a cockatoo, a brown snake—littered the area in a narrow line. As if a tendril of dark, sucking death had reached out to snatch at passing life. He realized it was not an old body, long forgotten, unknown. It was new; the clothes weren't weathered. The thing had taken it, taken the life from the man. When someone found the body, they'd think he died of thirst and hunger, all shriveled up like that. He thought of the little boy and the old lady who loved him, cared for him, who was family to him. He did not want that child's life stolen.

The light around him faded. Looking up, he could see the clouds closed over, and darkness formed around him. He wondered then, could the creature jump between pools of shadow or did it need a continuous channel of dark? Despite the questions, the logic, he felt the threat. The creature was close, hunger and darkness driving it. He flicked on the torch and shone it around him. It barely made a difference, so he flicked it off.

Jake didn't know what to do as the afternoon came and the shadows lengthened. Jake liked the dark. The thing that threatened him was not the dark itself but something that waited in the dark to steal life. He patted the torch, hoping it would be enough. He met Arlo and Birdie in the shadow of the outcrop. They shook their heads when he approached them.

'I found this,' Jake said as he held up the sock. Birdie's sharp intake of breath was enough confirmation.

'It's getting late, so keep your torches handy. I want you to come down through this section here, spread out but stay within shouting range. I'll keep my back to the outcrop so you should be able to locate me at short notice.'

Jake glided between the low-lying scrub and carefully stepped over fallen branches. He gritted his teeth at the sound of Birdie and Arlo crunching through the bush.

'Lee!' he called out.

When he found a small sandshoe, he called out again, certain that he was close. He could feel that mind, that hunger, so the creature was close as well.

A whimper sounded close by and he knew it was the boy. 'Lee? Lee. I'm coming to get you,' he called out. There was an answering wail.

The muffled sounds of voices reached him. It was Birdie and Arlo not too far away. 'I found him!'

He jogged, pushing a branch out of his way, then pulled up short. The boy was up a tree about one hundred meters away. Not a very convenient spot for rescue and not a safe place to hide from the creature.

He sensed the mind behind the dark spot he'd been following and his gaze riveted to the dark patch of shadow at the base of the tree. It was alive, hungry, desperate. The clouds moved again. The light arrowed down through the trees and a shaft fell on the tree trunk where the boy was clinging. The slavering spot of dark pulled back, fearing the light.

A sound of leaves crunching drew Jake's attention. A couple of kangaroos bounded through the bush, followed closely by Birdie and Arlo. The boy, Lee, saw them and cried louder.

Birdie went to walk over to get him.

'No, wait. See that?' Jake said, pointing.

Birdie paused. Both he and Arlo shared a look and turned their gaze to the shady spot on the ground. The creature was featureless and formless. Its shadowed form rose up like a blob of liquid tar on the boil.

Two pairs of rounded eyes stared back at him. 'That's it?' Arlo choked out.

Jake nodded

Already the ground was dry and brown. In the surrounding area, the leaves fluttered down, already dead, and a trail of bull ants slowly filled up with casualties.

The creature was poised between them. This close Jake could feel its thoughts, feelings. It was hungry, afraid, angry, alone. It did not want to die. The light shifted again and the thing silently shrieked, sending a wave of emotion over Jake. Perhaps it didn't need to hear to track its prey. Maybe it could feel him, sense life, as he could sense it.

It was growing darker beneath the canopy of the trees. It would be dark there before the fall of night. They had to use the light while they could.

He pulled out his torch and switched it on. With a nod to the others, they did the same. 'Be ready,' he said.

A shaft of sunlight speared down, clearing a path to the tree. Jake saw his chance and darted across the space between them. He jumped at the trunk to where the boy clung. After a little bit of convincing, Lee let go the tree and clutched him tight. His little body shook. Jake clutched him awkwardly, checking the ground to make sure there was still a patch of light to land on.

He shone the torch at the base of the tree to make certain. 'Here, focus your torches here.' Arlo and Birdie turned their lights to the base of the tree, even though it was still bathed in sunlight. Jake dropped, clutching the boy to him.

With his feet on the ground, he sensed the creature all around him, waiting to suck out their lives. They were food, nothing more. The shadows lurched again and light and dark shifted like disco lights along the leaf litter. Jake ran quickly to follow the sunlit path. Arlo and Birdie kept their torches focused on them. The boy screamed as the shadow lunged. Turning back, Jake fumbled for the torch and shone it straight into the dark center. The creature recoiled a fraction, enough to give Jake space.

Jake took a dive with the boy and landed in a clearing where the sun beat down. Lee whimpered and Jake thought he might have been hurt. 'Let me see,' he said to the boy.

Arlo and Birdie retreated, stepping close to huddle with them. Their torches shone outward, bathing them in a ball of safe life.

Jake reeled from the sight. The toes on Lee's right foot were shriveled, dead. They had not saved the boy completely; some of him had been sacrificed to the creature. A wind came and shook the trees and darkness grew around them. He patted the boy on the head. Snot and tears covered the boy's dark face. 'I'll take you back to your grandmother, okay?' The boy nodded, his tears slowing.

To the others, he said, 'I'll call an ambulance and have them meet us at the gate near the oval. You know it?'

'Yep, we came in that way,' Birdie said.

Jake bent down and hoisted the boy on his back. They ran the distance, puffing and wheezing with the exertion of climbing the ridge and having that thing chasing them. Once full darkness was on them, the creature would have no restraint.

As they neared the clearing, he called out. 'We've found him. We have him.'

Pat climbed down the slope part way to meet them. 'My boy. My little boy. You are safe.'

They met and she clutched the boy to her chest, running her hands over him and checking everywhere to make sure he was whole. Her hands paused on his bare feet.

'I'm sorry. His toes. It got his toes.'

Pat held the boy's foot and cried. Wiping her tears, she said, 'He lost his toes. He could have lost his life.'

'I've called an ambulance. Best get him seen to.'

Pat nodded and Birdie and Arlo went to their belongings to pack up. Jake's phone beeped. He glanced at the screen quickly. The police were waiting for him and an ambulance had arrived at the same location.

The afternoon sun slid behind the hills. The colors around them darkened and the smells changed with the dew. Jake felt a shiver. He could still feel the creature, feel its hunger. It was still there; maybe it would always be there, loitering, waiting in the bush, in the dark clefts between the hills and in the crevices of valleys.

'It's not safe here. Not in the dark,' he said.

'Yes, I agree. You come with me, yes?' said Pat, clinging to her grandson while she walked with her rocking gait and part limped toward the car.

Jake thanked her. 'I have things I must do now.'

'You don't have to stay lost, you know.'

'What?' He stopped dead and gaped at her. How did she...

'You don't have to have your life stolen like your father's was. You can find your life, your heritage.'

Jake swallowed. He tried to forget that stuff, tried to make it seem like it didn't matter.

'I...er...'

After placing the boy in the car, she touched his hand. 'Look for me and I'll help you, okay? I'll help you get your life back.'

Nodding dumbly, Jake watched them pull out. He'd check with the hospital when he finished up here. There was a warm spot inside of him. Pat had kindled something, a hope, a possibility that there was more to who he was. The close encounter with the life stealer made him think it was time for him to find that which had been stolen.

ৡৡৡ

The police brought lots of equipment with them in a van. Harsh, powerful spotlights attached to a generator. Jake grinned at the sight of them. By night the body of the bushwalker was fully illuminated. He felt the creature out there still, circling, prowling. The darkness allowed it to roam freely, supping on little lives, letting them plop to the ground. Where did such a thing come from? How was it held in check? Fire, he thought to himself. A bushfire could run faster than it, could trap it in a swift change of wind. Nature kept it under control.

The creature came closer, held at bay by the bright lights. Jake stood watching silently, listening the chatter as the police and forensics examined the corpse and the scene, looking for signs of foul play.

A lone technician left the others, went out into the darkness beyond the closer trees to piss. Jake felt the creature move. Without thinking, Jake leaped up to the nearest stand holding a searchlight and swung it around.

The technician started in fright. 'Stupid pervert bastard!' he yelled as he tugged up his fly. 'Nearly pissed all over myself.'

'Sorry, thought I saw something.' Jake kept the light on the creature, heard it scream, felt it shrink, felt it skulk away, far away.

This story came about in a number of ways. Russell B. Farr was putting out an anthology of Australian vampire stories called Dead Red Heart, *which is where this story was originally published. I lived in Karabar overlooking the ridge that looms over a section of the Queanbeyan River. On sunny days you can see the shadows in the clefts and they move around as the sun moves and I thought, what if there was a creature that lived in that dark space? However, I couldn't write a story about an Australian vampire without acknowledging an Indigenous connection, as Australia's First Peoples have been here for thousands upon thousands of years. Nor did I wish to appropriate Aboriginal or Torres Strait Islander culture or identity. This is a fine line to walk down. However, the double meaning of The Life Stealer I think tries to acknowledge the impact of white colonialism and the Stolen Generation. I would like to acknowledge the traditional owners of the land where this story is set, the Ngunnawal people.*

Veg Out

By the time Devartra arrived at the restaurant, her friends were already eating their huge steaks. Bright red blood pooled and congealed, clinging to the limp remains of mesclun salad. She repressed a shudder and averted her eyes. She could almost hear the moan of the cow as they cut into the flesh, slice by slice. She nodded a hello, then sat down, leaving a space of two or three seats between herself and the rest of the party.

'Hi, Devi,' said Jake, her one-time fling, who still had that blond cuteness that had always attracted her. 'Why are you sitting over there?'

'Well, you're already eating...and I didn't want to disturb you all.'

The others said their hellos absently, as if just noticing her presence, and returned to their food before she had time to ask after their health.

Within minutes of Devartra sitting down, the waiter pulled up. She handed him a brown paper bag filled with organic vegetables. The waiter held them in his hand as if he was holding dirty laundry.

'Please ask the cook to steam those for me, and under no circumstances is he to add butter, honey, or any other condiments. I've brought my own as I have special dietary requirements,' she said. The waiter nodded numbly and headed back to the kitchen.

'So how was the movie? Did I miss much?'

Suzy spoke first, around a mouthful of rare rump steak, and her plump face bulged with its load. 'Shame you missed it, Dev. Why did you?'

Devartra shrugged. 'I'm not sure. Something about the title just didn't do it for me.'

'Right,' said Brett around his half-chewed, well-done T-bone. 'Like the title really spooked you or something?' He returned to his steak, his unwashed locks falling forward to conceal his expression.

'Something like that,' she answered. She looked at Jake for support, but he shrugged and kept eating. She sat and listened to their commentary about the movie and ended up convinced that she hadn't missed much.

When the vegetables arrived, she knew straight away by the aroma that they were tainted with animal products.

'Excuse me,' she said, as she tugged on the waiter's arm. 'But I said no condiments. Now my meal is ruined.'

'You must be mistaken,' explained the waiter with a sneer, removing her arm daintily from his. 'There are no condiments on your steamed vegetables.'

'Look. I don't want to argue with you. Just get the chef and we'll sort this out, okay?'

The waiter turned and headed back to the kitchen. Several other patrons were looking at her, but she was used to that. It seemed that people thought you were weird if you were careful about what you ate and stuck up for your rights.

The chef arrived panting, coated with a greasy sweat. 'What seems to be the problem?' he asked nervously as his gaze slid off her.

'My steamed vegetables have been ruined by some condiments containing animal products.'

'I assure you that I did not put any condiments on your food. Let me see.'

He lifted the bowl, examined the vegetables and then sniffed. 'Mmm...yes, you're right. I will make up a fresh batch for you. Can I make you some sauce or something special?'

'No thanks. I have this.' She pulled out a bottle of organic, first-pressed, virgin olive oil. He nodded and went back to the kitchen.

Devartra looked at her friends. They appeared to be appalled, fascinated and repulsed by turns.

Jake looked at her, barely repressing a shudder. 'Devi, how on earth do you do it? You know...live with all that stress worrying about food?'

'How do you do it?' she replied, a little riled. 'Live with all those chemicals and additives in your food? You may not be repulsed by the killing of helpless animals, but think about the pesticides that concentrate in the food chain, and think about what you're putting in your mouths. Even the lettuce you eat has been genetically modified. You know they put animal genes into plants, don't you? Just watching you eat makes me stressed.'

❧❧❧

The next weekend, Devartra spotted a new store that had just opened at the markets. It was an organic shop, full of organic food at a reasonable price. Their main brand name appeared to be NewCo Products, which claimed to produce one hundred percent organically grown foodstuffs. She filled her trolley and went home. The food came with an advertising flyer, which mentioned that there was an open invitation to visit one of their farms. The date for the farm visit was the next day, Sunday.

After arriving home, she checked her answering machine, gazing into the hall mirror as she listened to the messages. She looked at her reflection and felt depressed. Her friends had rung while she was out to call off their Sunday outing. Then her eyes flashed with excitement, as she realized that she was now free to tour the NewCo farm.

On Sunday morning, she got up early and ate her rolled oats with organic soy milk. In preparation for her outing, she washed an organic apple in filtered water and then wrapped it in brown paper. In her trusty VW Beetle, she checked the map on the flyer, navigated down the highway and then turned off onto a rural dirt road.

When she arrived, it seemed as if she was the only one to take up the tour invitation. A flapping sound caught her attention. When she looked around, she saw a piece of paper fixed by a pin to the side of a dilapidated shed. She headed over for a closer look and stopped with a start when she heard the crunch of boots on the gravel.

An old guy turned the corner and smiled when he saw her, showing his yellow, gaping teeth. His clothes were dirty and he smelled none too clean. He introduced himself as Walpole. 'Yep...I'm the caretaker round here. Come for the tour I see...well, no-one but you's turned up. May as well walk around the wheat farm by yourself.'

'Okay, thanks,' replied Devartra and cast her gaze around the fields. 'Can I look at the corn fields or other types of vegetables?'

'Nope...you'll have to settle for the wheat fields. Nothing else is open to visitors. Just head back down the drive a ways and take a left at the second gate. You'll see it soon enough.'

He coughed, a chesty wheeze that made his already rough and red skin deepen to purple. Then he spat a huge glob of phlegm just to Devartra's right. Her stomach gave a little heave. She was able to smile weakly and wave to his retreating back.

Down the narrow rutted track, she drove until she found the second gate. The gate was heavy, but she managed to pull it open so she could drive inside. She pushed the gate shut, wiped her hands on her jeans and looked at the field. It went on and on. She walked along the access track, surrounded on both sides by acres of sun-browned wheat.

A breeze started up, and it shifted and billowed the wheat in crazy patterns. She stood for a while, fascinated, reveling in the pesticide-free space. Soon she would eat this wheat in her organic bread, a superior, organic bread. She walked through the fields, smiling at the sunshine and the natural beauty of the farm.

After walking for half an hour, she turned back to her car, and then heard the whispers. They sounded like a million *pisha-pishas* on the breeze. She stopped walking and looked around. There was no one there. She put her fingers in her ears and wiggled them around in case a bug had flown in to buzz and die in her ear canal.

It was quiet after she left her ears alone. She continued to gaze at the wind-caressed wheat. She took a few more tentative steps. Silence still reigned.

With a shrug, she quickened her pace and then faltered when she heard the whispers again.

'Killer! Killer!' the whispers said. Her jaw dropped. *No, it's just the wind*. Yet, it made her feel uneasy. Gooseflesh emerged on her arms and butterflies took flight in her stomach. The whispers grew more distinct. Words floated on the breeze. She ran back to her car, the sound of the hushed voices following her.

She snatched the door open and sat in her car, panting. She couldn't hear the whispers with the door shut. Eventually her heart and breathing slowed. She got out her apple and bit into it, chewing slowly and carefully. The wheat still rippled with the beat of the wind, but it was silent where she sat.

৯০৯০৯০

A weekend later, she was sitting at home bored. After walking around the garden and the interior of the house aimlessly, she decided to make a snack.

'Mmm...a touch of salad, perhaps,' she said to her budgie, Ralph. 'And if you're good you can have some too.'

After heaving the fridge door open, she leaned in and pulled out the lettuce, tomatoes and cucumber, and assembled them on the kitchen bench. She tore the lettuce and put it in the salad bowl, and slipped a leaf into Ralph's cage. Then she reached for a tomato.

Tilly, her tabby cat, distracted her by rubbing against her legs. 'What do you want, little puss?' she said, kneeling down to pat it. The cat purred contentedly and she let it go outside.

Returning to the kitchen bench, she reached for a sharp knife and plunged it into the tomato. There was a squeal—the sound of a stuck pig. She dropped the knife in shock, and it clattered to the floor, barely missing her feet.

Her hands trembled while she looked around, trying to find an explanation for the sound. Everything was quiet. The clock ticked and that was all she could hear. There was no easy explanation for the squeal that she'd heard.

She leaned in close and examined the tomato. It had a slight wound that seeped red tomato juice. She touched it with her finger, but there was no further sound. She let out a big sigh and relaxed, although she couldn't bring herself to use that tomato.

She got another one from the bag and washed it. It felt firm and smooth and it was unblemished. She sniffed it and it smelt good. She placed it on the wooden chopping board and sliced it. The tomato squealed, a terrible sound, and then was silent. From the bag of tomatoes, she heard nervous snorting and squealing and the paper rustled. She backed away from the kitchen bench and dropped the knife again. It stuck point first into the cork floor tiles, vibrating at the handle end.

A whimper escaped her, and then another. All of a sudden, she wasn't sure if she was sane anymore. How could she be perfectly rational one minute and stark raving mad the next?

She calmed down eventually, and placed the tomatoes in the corner. She couldn't decide what to do with them, but knew for certain that she couldn't eat them. As she was placing the bag in the corner, she noticed the brand name, NewCo Products, and in front of the computer code was some small writing. The writing was small and difficult to read, so she rummaged around, looking for a magnifying glass. She remembered her old chemistry set, so she went to the garage to find it. It took her half an hour to locate it amongst the spider webs, dirt and debris.

Wielding her dusty magnifying glass, she pulled the packet out into the light and looked at the lettering. The lettering stated that the product was one hundred percent organically grown-type...then nothing. The words were chopped off.

'Darn!' she yelled, and her voice echoed in the empty house. She went to the pantry and pulled out all the NewCo packets that she had bought. They had similar cut-up product information. She stalked over to the fridge, yanked it open and jumped when the door crashed into the wall. From the crisper, she pulled the other packets and placed them on the bench. The cut-off was different. Other words were visible, as if they had started where the others ended. She saw the word 'mod'. Gathering all the packets into a pile, she began to piece them together.

In the evening, Jake came by to visit her and watched a video with her. She didn't mention her weird experiences. In fact, she tried to forget the voices and sounds she had been hearing. She managed to conceal her disquiet, but could do little to disguise her rumbling stomach. After Jake complained about her bodily noises, she ate some leftover boiled rice. He left, giving her a platonic kiss on the cheek, and she went to bed.

The next morning, she ate her rolled oats and stared at the NewCo packaging piled on the bench, mulling over the product information. Picking one up, she twisted and turned it in different ways and noticed that the organic certification looked different too. Part of the logo caught her eye and she was able to piece together a word. 'GEN-MOD' formed after she placed four edges together. She sucked in her breath. The food produced by NewCo was genetically modified, and she couldn't believe it. How did that happen? The soil was organic, the fertilizers and insecticides were organic, but the plant stock was gen-mod. It was a mockery...it couldn't be true.

She jumped on the internet and looked up the company and information on genetically modified food. Eventually, she found a reference to porcine genes in tomatoes—there were pig genes in the tomatoes. It wasn't on the company site, though. She glanced over to the bag of tomatoes. They made pig noises...it had to be true. But how had she heard them? Was she psychic? Thinking back to the farm visit, the strange whispers, she wondered what was in the wheat. Human genes? When would they stop breaching the species divide?

She rang the company's customer service line, and a recorded message said that the line was unattended. She paced around the kitchen and looked at the tomatoes sitting in the corner. Doubt clouded her mind. It was so hard to believe that she decided to check again. She pulled out another ripe tomato and cut it. It squealed, and she jumped. *This can't be happening*, she thought. She ran to the toilet and retched. Even if they were genetically modified, she wondered why she was hearing them. She certainly didn't want to hear them.

The next day, she contacted the company and asked them about their products. She kept her voice mild as the customer service woman assured her that no chemicals were used in the production and that the soil was regularly tested for residue. The customer service woman didn't mention the genetically modified seed.

'So how do you get the food to look so perfect?' she said, trying to coax some information out of her. 'It's like you have special seeds or something.'

The lady replied that they were very happy with their product and they used a disease-resistant strain to maximize yields without the use of chemical fertilizers and pesticides.

'So you don't use genetically modified seeds, do you?' Devartra asked. The lady on the other end was quiet. Devartra could hear the woman shuffling papers. The woman then advised her to make her inquiry in writing to head office, as she could not answer any more questions. 'Too technical,' she said and hung up.

Devartra was left with the phone in her hand, listening to the dial tone with suspicions multiplying by the second.

Later that day, she decided to drive out to the NewCo farm. She waited until late afternoon so she would arrive under the cover of dark. She drove slowly on the dirt road with her headlights switched off. She reached the gate, pulled up and got out of the car.

All she could hear was the wind as it moved the plants and rattled the fences. She jumped the fence and landed with a quiet thump. Walking with her torch pointed down, she heard the plants whispering when she neared the fields,

'Killer, killer...' She shivered and hugged herself with her free arm, as her tears rolled down her cheeks.

'God, stop it!' she cried out. She wanted to block them out, didn't want to believe it.

Startled by a barking dog, she raced back to the fence, jumped over it and hurried into the car. The sound of the engine humming blocked out the sound of the wheat's accusing whispers. Putting the car into reverse, she maneuvered down the track and went home.

৵৵৵৵

Immediately, she stopped buying NewCo Products and tried others. At first, everything was fine. Then, as the weeks passed, other fruit and vegetables made noises. It was as if the genetically modified food was spreading to other plants, to conventionally grown foods.

She ate only imported rice and water and as time wore on she became very thin.

Jake called in to see her. 'Devi! What's the matter? Are you ill?'

'No...what makes you say that?' she replied, eyes shifting and feet shuffling. 'I'm fine... nothing wrong with my mind.'

'But you're so thin. You're overly obsessed about food. Let me get you something or take you out.'

'No...it's the same everywhere. The genetically modified food—it's in everything. I can tell.'

'What rubbish are you on about now? Geez, Devi, you can be such a babe, but when you carry on about food I glaze over. Enough already. I'll make you a tea.'

'No!' she shouted. 'I can't.'

'Devi?' Jake said, staring at her. He walked up to her and tried to get her to look into his eyes. But she shut them, shut him out.

'You won't even look at me. I thought we were friends.'
Jake left, slamming the door behind him.

Silence. Aloneness.

Devartra sat back down on the couch, huddled into a ball and stared into space. She couldn't tell him what was wrong. She didn't want to lose her only good friend. Everyone would remember...Did you hear that Devi had an episode? Yeah, heard the veggies talking. Quite bizarre actually. Always knew she was a loony, always prating on about not eating meat and toxins in the food.

Yet, despite the fear of ridicule, she knew that she couldn't go on like this, or she would get sick and die. There was definitely something happening with the food, and she decided to do something about it.

After Jake left, she rang the NewCo Products' customer service line.

'Listen. The tomatoes squeal like pigs when I cut them. I'm a vegan. I can't eat products with animal substances in them. You're using genetically modified products.'

She paused and realized that she had been talking to the dial tone. The woman had hung up before she had finished her first sentence. Devartra was getting desperate. She screamed defiantly into her mirrored reflection.

She paused. The person in the mirror couldn't be her. Pale skin, sunken cheeks, black rings around staring dark eyes. Staggering back, she ran outside. The sounds were there too. Even the grass whispered to her, about her.

There was nowhere she could hide.

She stopped going to work. She tried a few times, but dashed into bushes, only to tear out of them a second later when they whispered. The grass whispered...'Killer, killer...'

At first, she didn't understand, and then the penny dropped. Wheat was a type of grass—no wonder it had spread. While she stood dazed, a neighbor walked by and enquired after her health. Devartra started, and then cringed.

She scrambled back inside her house and shut the door, crouching, waiting. The light flashed on her answering machine, but she didn't replay the messages. She had stopped returning her friends' calls.

What could she say? Come over and have a chat with Mr. Corn Cob. He has a very interesting perspective on life. She sobbed as the thought passed through her mind. She couldn't go on like this, something had to give.

In a final attempt to see justice done, she called up her local member of parliament and confessed it all. She told him about NewCo Products, about the wheat whispering and the tomatoes squealing. She told him about all the noises, and how the genetically modified food was cross-pollinating and getting into the normal food chain. The member of parliament talked soothingly to her and asked her about where she lived, assuring her that he would look into it.

She cried into the phone with relief. 'Thank you-thank you-thank you,' she said as she sobbed. Now, she thought, it would stop and there would be an end to her torture. Now they would put a stop to the propagation of genetically modified food. But could they stop it now it had spread? It was so hard to think...it had been so long since she had eaten properly. She was still crying and talking on the phone when there was a knock at the door. She stopped suddenly.

'C...can you hold a minute? There is someone at the door....' Her heart beat frantically and she looked for somewhere to hide.

'I'll wait, dear. Why don't you go and answer it? It won't take a minute.'

'Answer it? You want me to answer the door...but...'

'No...you don't have to answer the door if you don't want. I just wanted you to know that I'd still be here if you did.'

'Okay...I understand. Please wait a minute...'

Uncurling herself from the couch, she crept down the hall and opened the door. Two uniformed policemen stood there. Her mouth hung open as they reached for her. She had no strength to fight.

'Don't worry, miss,' said the large one with sad brown eyes.

'Yes, don't worry, we'll take you somewhere safe. Come on, luv, don't struggle now,' said the smaller one, who didn't smile. His name tag said Officer Milton.

'No. It's not me. It's that NewCo product. They put genetically modified food into our food chain.' In the background, the grass whispered. 'Can't you hear it too? I don't want to hear them, but for some reason they speak to me.'

'Quiet now, miss. Won't be long now,' said Officer Milton as he placed her in the car and slid in next to her. Tears fell down her cheeks, and she looked out the car window feeling helpless. The grass swayed, the daisies nodded and she heard the grass whisper through the open window, 'killer, killer, killer...', as she was driven away in the squad car.

She wrung her hands; they were very thin. Glancing at her arms, she noted they looked like sticks. She sighed. Soon there would be nothing she could eat. She didn't eat animal products, couldn't bring herself to do so.

They thought she was nuts, but she knew better. Soon there would be no divide between plants and animals.

'God, I hope I'm dead before then,' she said under her breath.

'What's that, miss? Want to harm yourself, do you?' Officer Milton said as he made notes in his little notebook.

ঔঔঔ

Devartra staggered into the lounge. A psychiatric nurse nodded to her and Devartra went to the window. There was solid concrete in the patio. There was concrete all around the hospital, so she felt safe here. She no longer heard the whispers.

'Devi?' the nurse called. She shuffled over and paused. Uncertain, she was sure she had heard that familiar sound. Another step, then another. The closer she got the more distinct the whispers sounded. She stopped and gasped.

'Come on, Devi. I won't hurt you. I've got something for you. Come on,' said the nurse, beckoning with her hand. Devartra took a few more steps and neared the nurse's station. The whispers were growing louder. It had been so long since she had heard that sound. She was better, they had said. Cured, even. Medication, forced feeding and rest were all she had needed, and she was going home on the weekend.

A low moan escaped her as the whispers got louder and clearer. She wasn't mad! She was sane!

As she edged closer, the nurse lifted up a pot plant of chilies and said, 'These are for you. They've just been delivered.'

This is one of my earlier stories. I was a vegetarian at the time I wrote this, but not a vegan. My then partner was flirting with the idea of becoming one and I found it to be too strict and didn't want to be one. Not that there is anything wrong with vegans! My daughter is now a vegan and she is appalled by this story. The idea for the pig genes in tomatoes came from a New Scientist *article about pig genes being put in tomatoes. It seemed like in those days that scientists would swap genes around for the fun of it. You know, fluorescent jelly fish genes in monkeys and so on to see if they would glow in the dark. And then there were all those cross-pollination stories of genetically modified grains infecting non-genetically modified crops. It came to my mind that if they put animal genes in vegetables, what would the vegetarians eat? Then the idea of squealing tomatoes arrived and there you go. Also, I meant this to be a serious horror piece, but some have read it as a comedy.*

A Vagabond Rhyme

Two hundred rows of green, jagged-leafed grape vines spread out around me. I stop to fondle a bunch of grapes, not quite ripe but filled with potential. Their symmetry is perfect. My gaze drifts to another bunch even larger and fuller, the fruit tinged with red. I lose myself here amongst the vines that whisper and soothe.

Another few steps and I turn into another row, still lost in my meanderings. My dog near trips me as he pounces on a blade of grass. Memories and odd thoughts scatter as I find my balance and curse my pet for my own clumsiness. White and fluffy, he bounds playfully away, chasing a bird or a cricket.

A rural fence disguised by rough scrub and overgrown shrubs is interrupted by the gate and the green-painted mail tin. *What will come?* I wonder as I head down the drive. A bill that assures me that I exist and someone knows I'm here? These acres are lonely now that Sam is gone. My sigh lingers on the breeze until it is disturbed by a flock of cockatoos screeching as they lift off from the vines.

A small cloud shadows the sun, cloaking the past. Sunlight reflecting off an envelope winks at me from afar. I smile to myself and then jerk to a stop. My pleasure leaks away. There's a man on the other side of the gate. He wears big boots, dust brown and full of holes. His big toe sticks out. Old work boots. His jeans are dark blue with white cotton frays around serrated cuts and the knees are black like he's been praying in newly laid bitumen. I pause, heart thumping. In this place people aren't usually at the gate. They motor up the driveway or they ring first so you know they are coming. Not loitering. Not watching. Waiting.

My hands clench as I swallow the spit in my mouth. Maybe he'll move on. But he doesn't. He watches me with pale grey eyes staring out of a dirty, tanned face. He has a beard, not long or short but unkempt, unruly like my thoughts, and there's a knapsack on the ground leaning against his calf. My heartbeat thuds in my chest painfully. Should I turn back and fetch the mail later? I hesitate, caught in my palpitation. He doesn't speak, only watches with those eyes. As I get nearer I see his lips are moving; he's reciting something, rambling. Oh god! A nutter! I stop again.

'Go away!' It comes out of my mouth automatically. I'm surprised by how hard my voice is, how inflexible I am.

He keeps mumbling, but his eyes shift to mine. His hand outstretches in supplication. I see he's thin, his cheeks sunken. I should feel pity. I turn back, instead. His words become clearer as I walk stiff-backed. They swarm like bees around my head and ears. The dog charges the gate, a low growl at the ready. The dog doesn't bark, though, and goes quiet. Rotten bugger! I hope the beggar is not petting my traitor dog.

That night, the vision of the beggar comes to me in my dreams. Is he hungry? Is he cold? Is he lonely? It's not my business, I tell myself. I put a pillow over my head and go back to sleep.

❧❧❧

Cockatoos call raucously to each other while bobbing on the end of branches as I head to the mail box the next morning. My mail is still there and the man is gone, moved on, whatever. I unlatch the gate and scream. He is there again. Not moved from the day before. Due to the angle of the drive and the shrubs, I didn't see him. The words he utters float around him. Poems. He is reciting poetry. Shakespeare, John Donne, Dylan Thomas and Wordsworth.

Random stanzas and lines intermixed. Our eyes meet. I can't breathe.

He says, 'Keep up your bright swords, for the dew will rust them—She, she is dead; she's dead; when thou know'st this, Thou know'st how dry a cinder the world is—Before you let the sun in, mind it wipes its shoes—Dear God! The very houses seem asleep...'

I stand there not sure what to do. Gate half open, dog now pushing against my calves, the mail in the box and him weaving poetry in the air. Strangely, I feel calm. I don't feel threatened. Perhaps it's the poetry falling from his mouth like a prayer. The dog surges forward and licks the man's boots. The man's eyes smile, his voice quietens. I lunge for the mail and sag when I see the logo. It's the rates. The goddamn rates!

'I can give you a meal if you want. But that's all. You have to go after that.' I've said enough to assuage my guilt. I'm still not involved.

The man smiles, dirty brown teeth. 'Busy old fool, unruly sun, Why dost thou thus, through windows, and through curtains call on us.'

I resist the urge to roll up my eyes. Metaphysical poetry before lunch. He shuts the gate, pats the dog's fluffy head and ruffles his ears. This vagabond, this hobo, this street person is coming into my home. I feel like calling the police, but I don't.

There's not much food in the house. I open the pantry and finger a can of baked beans. No problem giving him that. It's nutritious, wholesome and boring. Do I want to go to the effort of making something nice? No. That's too welcoming. It's not like I need the company. I have my memories for that.

He shovels the baked beans into his mouth, dripping sauce on his beard. He wipes the dribbles with the back of his hand. 'He's an absent-minded beggar and his weaknesses are great.' The smile is back in his eyes. He must be crazy.

He pulls out a book from his bag, a tatty, olive-green hard cover. He starts to read. 'I could not dig: I dared not rob, therefore I lied to please the mob—Virtue could see to do what Virtue would by her own radiant light, though sun and moon were in the flat sea sunk.'

Kipling and Milton? I almost gag at the combination. I sort socks and towels in an effort to block him out. Shakespeare again and is that Wordsworth? It's woven through, laughably cobbled together, as if he's reading three poems simultaneously.

I hike out to the line and peg out the clothes. The wind is up. The birds dart overhead, heading to the shelter of the pines. I think I hear the man's poetry like an undercurrent in the wind.

෧෧෧

I add more butter to the potatoes and give them a final whip with the fork. I've not seen the strange poet, the vagabond, for a while. I check the sausages on the grill and turn to pull out a plate. I jump back. He's there again. 'Dear god, don't scare me like that!'

He smiles at me, the skin crinkling around the eyes. He's clean. I look down and see the dog is, too. They must have been to the dam.

I look away to the dinner, enough for two. 'Are you hungry?' I ask and point to the table. He moves off and the dog follows him, tail wagging.

Eating together at the same table is unnerving. His green hardback book is on the table beside him. He eats distractedly, his eyes returning to the pages. I wonder what I should do with him. It is late. The wind has brought rain, heavy rain. It drums on the tin roof like nervous fingers insinuating tension into the house. The study was far enough away from me. Perhaps he could....

He finishes his meal and stands while pushing the plate forward. He rattles off a few lines of poetry by Lord Tennyson. 'She left the web, she left the loom, she made three paces through the room.'

My eyebrows knit. This is ridiculous. 'You can stay in the study. There's a single bed in there.'

He nods and the dog leads him away. There's no telly. I try to sleep but I stare into the open closet, where my husband's clothes still hang. My eyes linger on the shadows, knowing all those little things that belonged to Sam are still there. I throw off the blankets and begin to go through the wardrobe. I pull some clean clothes out, fold a shirt, trousers and the rest. I edge open the door and peek out. The study door is shut, but the murmur of poetry still leaks through the cracks. I step closer and lay the pile of clothes down.

The next morning the sun is already soaking up the rain puddles. The blue sky is flawless like a sapphire I once had set in a ring. I rummage through the fridge for a picnic lunch and a bottle of last year's vintage. The screen door bangs as I step outside.

The forest is peaceful. I lie back on my red-checked blanket. The sun leaches the green away; the leaves on the gums fade to grey. I hear the poet again. He's there behind me, dressed in my Sam's old clothes. They make him look whole and less of a lunatic. I start and upset my wine. Hesitantly I offer him food. He touches my hand when he accepts the sandwich. My gaze falls upon the book. I can't make out the title. I look away to the forest, the trees marching back until they become obscure and mesh into a dark grey blur.

I see movement, like a person walking behind a tree. Sitting forward, I stare hard, watching for it again. Out of the corner of my eye I see something. My eyes focus on three women walking in the wood. Flowing Grecian-style gowns of white, cinched at the waist with gold sashes, hair half bound in a bun, with the remainder trailing like waves of auburn down their backs. They are beautiful; I can see it even from this distance. Skin like alabaster, eyes dark, red wine-colored lips.

I shake my head, thinking the scene is a pantomime rehearsal. One of the women touches a tree trunk with a graceful hand, trailing her fingers on the bark. Then she steps lightly and surely to weave a path among the eucalypts.

Then I see a man. He's in a blue business suit. I blink back my surprise and scramble to my feet. I hear the poetry in the air yet am alone on my blanket. I jog part way into the forest, leaping the creek and almost catching my foot on a loose stone.

I can smell these women; a tantalizing perfume floats in the air and my mouth waters. There are more men following these women. I tread further, engrossed in watching them. The women stride effortlessly without appearing to hurry.

The first man is running, but he hasn't caught the one he's chasing yet. I can hear him panting. It echoes around me, growing louder. I see the woman smile and turn partially back. The man is close to her; he reaches out to touch her.

I watch, biting my tongue. The man screams. He's staring at his hand. It's mottled purple and blisters are forming. The more he screams the more the blisters spread. His hand is gnarled now and his chest is bubbling, the flesh roiling as if drowning in acid. My eyes dart to the other men. 'Don't!' I shout, starting to run. 'Don't touch them.'

No one listens to me. The other men are pursuing the women with even more haste. I hear screams and know more are being hurt. I run deeper into the forest. Again I hear the poet's words on the breeze, meaningless jumbles of rhymes. I look back but I can't see him, or the picnic or the grass where I was sitting. I hear footsteps. Another man approaches. 'Don't touch them!' I yell into his face. But his eyes are glazed.

I bury my head in my hands and bend over double, sucking breath into my lungs. I hear feet treading purposefully toward me, the crunching of leaves and twigs. I look up. A man is approaching me. But he's not an ordinary man. He walks slowly toward me, and I am spellbound. He is Apollo, Adonis, a god amongst men. His white robe flows around him. The sleeves of the short tunic contrast with his tanned arms.

A spicy smell reaches me. I inhale it deeply. I can't move. I feel no fear. His face is serene. Soft brown curls brush against his temple and cheek. His eyes are dark like midnight without stars. I stare into them, searching for a sprinkling of stardust. His soft hand strokes my cheek, and I shiver with excitement. His expression never changes. His perfectly shaped mouth is opening. I see the neatly formed teeth as he draws me closer. My mouth is open and eager. I want him to kiss me. He captures my mouth and kisses me hungrily.

I am transformed by the taste of him. I am ravenous. My passion rises, thrilling my blood with desire. My juices flow in anticipation. I want to give myself to him completely. I don't care if I live or die.

My skin is singing with the joy of his touch. We make love. I am sighing and groaning and screaming with ecstasy. His caresses, his movements, seem to go on forever. I'm lost in it, fulfilled by it. I weep with bliss. This man-god has touched my very soul. Our rhythm peaks. I don't want the moment to end. I want to cling. I want to hold him forever. And then he is gone.

My enlivened senses, the nerve endings in my skin, are throbbing. I breathe through it and open my eyes. The forest is gone. He is gone. I want to wail at his abandonment. But I notice something about where I am. A room that is familiar. My brain kicks in, sifting through images trying to find the correct name for the place and the time. I touch my abdomen. I'm pregnant...very pregnant and sitting on a couch. My mouth hangs open while I try to comprehend, and then my first husband walks in.

I scream. I am in my past. Terror assails me. I don't want to live through that time again. I scream louder. 'What are you doing, you stupid girl?' says my first husband. His words cut me. They bring back all the pain and hurt of that time. The past that I had buried so deep is now an open wound. I want to cry but the tears are afraid to fall. He never liked weeping women.

Desperation near overwhelms me. I hear the poetry in the air. Soothing. If I am back in my past, perhaps I can change it.

I feel a wave of dizziness and the room around me blurs and shifts. I open my eyes. Once more the place is familiar. It is the past again, but another part of my life filled with humiliation and personal trials. 'No!' I cry, 'I don't want to do this again.' I fear the degradation and all those things that made my life hurt back then. I fight it. Nothing seems to shift, and then I remember that those painful things made me what I am now, they made me grow, made me strong. My fear falls away.

Again my vision wavers, yet I am at peace. Whatever is thrown at me I know I can conquer it, for I have conquered it before.

A breeze shifts my hair. The call of lorikeets and currawongs stir the air. I smell the grass and the dust and open my eyes once again. I am in the forest where the vision began. The women are gone. So is the man. How I long for his touch, the thrill of his mouth on mine. I sigh. Lovemaking never felt like that.

I feel tenderness between my legs and pause. A slow trickle leaks out of me and dampens my underpants. My skin feels enlivened as it did under his touch. My blood pulses energetically. I step on stones to cross the creek. My dog is there, asleep on the blanket. The spilled bottle of wine makes a puddle in the corner of the rug. Sitting square on the blanket is the tattered green book. The title was once embossed in gold. I finger it, tracing my nails along the indents. It was called *A Vagabond Rhyme*.

I flick it open and thumb a few pages. The lines of famous poems are intermingled, just as the hobo had said them. One line stands out above all others. Shakespeare, I think it is. 'I have had a dream, past the wit of man to say what dream it was.'

Back at the house I feel different. My home is no longer a hallowed place, a shrine to my memories. It is a burden, a reminder that I have refused to move forward. I swing open the wardrobe and pack my things. When I am done, I pick up the tattered green hardback and put it in the car. My dog leaps onto the back seat, tongue lolling. I steer the car down the drive, leaving the grapes loaded with a potential harvest.

With some regret I pause, but the links to the past are too strong: wines, grapes, sweat, death...

A swirl of dust rises up as my tires leave the drive. With the book next to me, I smile. It is my turn to quote *The Vagabond Rhyme*.

They say you shouldn't turn dreams into stories—this story came mostly from a dream. The poet side came from the theme of a short story competition I was aiming for. It didn't make the cut and I went on to have 'A Vagabond Rhyme' published elsewhere. A few years later, I saw that it had received an honorable mention in the Australian Year's Best *for that year. I was very pleased about that. The story is set on the small vineyard where I was living at the time. Elements of this story are from my past and I feel that here I am thinking about things we hold onto from our pasts that prevent us moving forward.*

The Doctor's Pill

'Come in, Jane,' said Doctor Smiley. 'Take a seat over here next to me.' Doctor Smiley looked down at the open file on his desk. The notes read: Jane Simpson, eighteen years, four-year history of an eating disorder in conjunction with severe obsessive compulsive disorder pertaining to food and toilet habits. Hospitalized seven times. A letter on file from her general practitioner begging for some assistance before it was too late.

'Hmm.' He looked at Jane and estimated that she was five feet, four inches, probably five and a half stone or 35 kilos. He looked back down at the file; there were at least ten photos in the file: one of a laughing girl about 50 kilos, the rest images of Jane in various stages of emaciation. The nurse's scrawl showed her statistics and he smiled slightly—his guess had been spot on. Obviously, he had been at this too long.

'So, Jane, tell me: what can I do for you that hasn't been done already?'

Jane looked at him, her cheeks sunken and her eyes dull. 'Help me!' A tear escaped her eyes and she tried blinking it back. 'Every time I look in the mirror I see a fat person, but my family keep putting me in hospital. I try and eat and, when I do, I see fat and starve myself.'

'I see. And do you really believe I can help you?' He regarded her, waiting to see how willing she was to stop her cycle of starvation and bingeing.

Her dull grey eyes shifted uneasily and then she glanced at him quickly, unwilling to hold his gaze. She fidgeted and played with her hair. She didn't answer until he asked her again.

'Yes. You're my only hope.'

'Well…it happens that I may have something that will help you. However, I have to explain to you that it is a trial and there is no guarantee that the treatment will work.'

'Okay, I don't have any other choices.' She nodded and kept on nodding.

'You're sure?' As she kept nodding, he got out the paper work. There were five forms to sign: his indemnity, the practice indemnity, acknowledgment of the trial, waiver, and non-disclosure agreement. He stacked them in a neat pile and handed her a pen, and then buzzed the nurse to come and witness the signature. Luckily, Jane was old enough to sign, otherwise he'd have had to get her guardians to do it.

৵৵৵

Jane finished signing the forms and watched the nurse apply her squiggle. The nurse looked her up and down and then left. Jane stood up and walked around the room, carefully avoiding contact with any items. She pulled out a sani-wipe from her bag and wiped her hands. She had touched the pen, after all.

'Okay, Jane, come and sit down and I will explain it all to you.'

She sat down quickly; her heart was beating erratically as she realized that she had no idea what horrible treatment this doctor would prescribe. She'd already been to the 'poo farm' that fed her juices and piled in the enemas and hot water bottles in her rear to purify her; the sedation; the tube feeding. She'd done it all. What could be worse than that? Eating?

'Now, Jane—' he pulled out a large pink pill in a vial '— I want you to fill up that glass of water over there and bring it back here. Don't worry, it's been sterilized; just be careful when you undo the wrapper.'

She did as he asked and he passed the vial to her. 'Now, I want you to put the pill in your mouth and swallow. That's right, good girl.'

The pill was large and it made her gag, but it went down. Then she looked at the doctor as if he was a bug in a microscope. Was that it? She thought it was strange. She waited for him to explain. She sat for half an hour and he still said nothing.

'Good! That should be enough time for the pill to be absorbed. You won't be up-chucking it now.' She started when he spoke. He got up quickly and washed his hands. 'Come back and see me next month. If the treatment is working, we will know by then. Okay?'

He put his hand on her back and propelled her out the door. She stopped, digging in her heels. 'Is that it? Just a pill?'

'Yes, that's it. Radical treatment, but I am sure you can cope with that. It was painless, wasn't it?'

'Yeah, but how's it work?'

'I'm sorry, Jane. I am not at liberty to discuss it. It is a trial, after all, and I have signed an agreement with the drug company to keep the nature of the pill secret. I know it works with minimal side effects. If you feel there is a problem just come back—anytime.'

He shut the door and called his next patient. Jane was nudged out the way as the next patient tried to get through the door.

Jane paid her $250 non-refundable, non-claimable fee and left. She didn't care, as her mother had footed the bill. She mused that the doctor was the weirdest she had ever come across. She decided to try to throw the pill up. It might have calories or fat. It was unusual for her to put something like that in her mouth.

She passed two sets of public toilets; neither was suitable. She headed for the mall and went to her favorite cubicle. She pulled out five sani-wipes and wiped the seat, the toilet roll holder and the door knobs. Then she leaned over the toilet bowl and tried to puke. Only clear bile came out as a result of her near-silent regurgitation. She climbed upon the toilet seat, standing carefully on the toilet paper she had placed there.

She peed. One, two, three, hold, then four. Done. She rummaged through her purse and swallowed five laxatives. If she couldn't dislodge the pill she'd purge it before she had time to put on any weight.

The next morning she looked in the mirror. Standing naked, she turned slowly, noting the fat rolls and the bulges, the array of cellulite. She decided not to eat today—she was too fat.

That night she washed carefully in front of the mirror. She looked at her body first and saw the dark smears on her pale skin. He, her father, had touched her there long ago, but she could still see the marks. She was still unclean.

Using pre-boiled water in a sterile bowl—the shower was full of germs and she never used it—she lathered the antiseptic soap all over her body, pushing it in her rear, her vagina, her nostrils and her mouth. She rinsed them out when the burn became unbearable. She used her douche and felt the hot water cleanse her.

There was a knock. 'Fuck off!' she yelled, and she was answered by a curse. She loaded the douche again, felt the antiseptic cleanse her, and it made her shudder with purity. Then she did her nostrils. The water poured out of her mouth and burned her throat.

She was clean.

She panted, and she glowed. She turned on the heat lamps and waited for an hour for her skin to dry. She looked at herself closely in the mirror. Her vagina fascinated and repulsed her. Her pubic hairs were growing back. She would need to wax them again.

She opened the door and walked naked to her room. Her brother spat a curse, 'Christ, Jane, do you have to do that? You look like a corpse. Your tits have totally sunken down to nothing. I think I'm gonna puke.'

She slammed her door and panted on the other side. She laid the tissue paper over her bed and lay down. The light blared brightly. She kept her eyes open as long as possible as it helped keep her pure.

She was hungry the next morning. She ate five slices of toast, four rashers of bacon, three fried eggs, two cups of coffee and one orange juice. Then she ran to the bathroom and stripped off her clothes.

She saw herself perfectly thin in the mirror, her perfect flat breasts, bald vagina and thin legs. Perfect.

She went to school and didn't eat lunch and when she returned she went straight to the bathroom. She looked in the mirror and she was fat and disgusting again. She cried, remembering how perfect she had seemed that morning. She raced to the fridge and stuffed her face with leftover chicken, baked potatoes and gravy. Her mother found her on the floor with the fridge open and legs splayed apart.

Jane got up and raced out of the room when she heard her mother's distressed call. She locked herself in the bathroom and waited. She paced, trying to estimate how many laxatives she needed to take to counteract the food she had just stuffed in her mouth.

She stripped of her clothes and performed her cleansing ritual. She double douched everywhere, including her eyes and ears. As she stood under the heat lamp, she turned her gaze to the mirror. She looked perfect. Her thin body was like a gentle reed, supple, willowy, everything she wanted it to be.

She went to bed and slept. The next morning she was hungry, and she ate her breakfast in the same numerical order. Then she ran to the bathroom and stripped off— her body was still perfect. She smiled and left for school.

Her routine continued and at the end of the month she returned to the doctor's surgery. He looked up at her when she entered, smiled vaguely, then returned to his notes.

'Mmm. That's right, you're a trial patient. How's things with you?'

Jane smiled brightly, her eyes glowing with health.

Jane saw him note down that her breasts were firm and her hips rounded. The doctor estimated that she was now 50 kilos. He wrote a few notes down in her file and checked his estimate with the nurse's statistics.

'Spot on again,' he mumbled to himself, and then looked up with a start when Jane spoke.

'I'm very well, doctor. I don't think I need to come again.'

'Well. I know you think everything is fine, but you must come back next month. That is part of the agreement you signed. Remember?'

Jane didn't remember, but she nodded anyway and left. She paid her bill and went home. Her mother had been so nice and even her brother's friends were talking to her, as if they liked her instead of treating her as a freak.

The months went by and soon she became disturbed by her brother's comments and her mother's strange looks. The words obese, fat pig and grotesque floated in the air at home, at school and in the street. She couldn't understand it. When she took off her clothes, she saw that her body was perfect. She was cured.

Her mother was upset and showed her the labels on the new clothes: size 18 and size 20. They had an argument and Jane accused her of trying to drive her crazy—she wasn't fat. Then Jane had a seizure and they called the ambulance.

Doctor Smiley opened the door and ushered Jane in; he had to step back to let her pass. 'Come in, Jane, have a seat by the desk. You are looking well, dear.'

'Doctor, they said I was obese!'

'Well, I wouldn't say that exactly. You're just not thin anymore. You wanted a cure and it looks like you have one.'

'Doctor, I had a heart attack. The emergency doctor said I had to diet or the fat around my heart would kill me. Tell me it's not true! I can't believe it. My body is perfectly thin.'

Doctor Smiley wrote hurriedly in his notes. 'I see. That is interesting. Are you eating normally now? No more toilet habits?'

'I eat good meals and a few snacks now and then. I don't worry about cleaning the toilet anymore and I only do some of my cleansing rituals.'

His eyebrow lifted, a ray of grey and white. 'So you think that you are cured?'

'Yes, doctor, but I am afraid. I don't look fat, but the doctor showed me the evidence.'

Doctor Smiley stood up and paced, his hand idly scratching his chin. 'This is unprecedented. I wonder what would happen if I gave you another pill.' He went to the cupboard and got another pink pill down. Then he wrote furiously in his notes. He eyed Jane warily. 'Mmm, I estimate that you are now over 100 kilos. I think you are sufficiently cured to stabilize to a normal routine.' As if hedging all his bets he handed her the pill.

She took it eagerly, swallowed it without water, her puffy mouth closing juicily over the large pill. She stood up and thanked the doctor and left.

The next morning, Jane screamed. She saw herself in the mirror. She had huge breasts and she couldn't see her vagina as her stomach hung down so low. Her rear was encased in two huge cheeks filled with sweat and muck. Her face when she screamed was like an oversized purple grape. She could see reality. How things really were. She no longer saw what she wanted to see and she didn't like it.

❧❧❧

A couple of weeks later two policemen, Officer Digby and Officer Wilberforce, called to see Doctor Smiley. He sat back in his chair and placed his reading glasses over his nose.

'Sorry to disturb you, doctor. Just a few questions regarding Jane Simpson,' said Officer Digby.

The doctor buzzed the nurse and requested Jane's file. 'Has something happened to Jane?'

Officer Wilberforce spoke and the doctor turned his gaze to him. 'She's dead. Suicide.'

'Oh! That's terrible. How did she do it? She had a bad heart, you know.'

'She choked to death on food. In front of her family.'

'Oh, that's bad. How can I help you? I don't think I can shed any light on the matter.'

'You were treating her, weren't you, doctor?' asked Officer Digby.

'Yes, for an eating disorder and other related conditions. However, she was cured.'

'May we know the nature of the cure, doctor? You see, she left a note,' prompted Officer Digby.

'Did she now? Well, I cannot divulge the nature of her treatment, as she signed waivers to that effect. The nurse will give you a copy of the waiver on your way out.'

'You don't want to know what the note said?' asked Officer Wilberforce, unable to keep the surprise from his face.

'Oh, I know what the note said.'

Both officers sat straighter in their chairs, 'What!' they said in unison.

'The note said, 'It worked'.'

'But how could you know that?' said Officer Digby as he wrote hurriedly in his notebook.

'Just a lucky guess. Now, if you will excuse me, I have a lot of patients to see. Good day to you.'

Doctor Smiley shut the door after the officers and sat down for a nice cup of tea. He noted in Jane's file the event of her death and then wrote a note to the drug company recommending a second pill when the subject returned to ideal weight.

His nurse buzzed, announcing his next patient. Her name was Jill Howard, she was eighteen, long history of eating disorders. He flicked through the various snap shots and saw the general practitioner's letter begging for help.

'Come in, Jill. Come and sit by me.'

This is another one of my earlier stories, written when I really didn't know much about what I was doing. On looking over some of these stories, it does appear that I have an issue with doctors and with drug companies, too. I was also interested in the harm that happens to people when they are molested or abused as children or have issues with fitting in. Sometimes just existing can be hard. 'The Doctor's Pill' garnered an honorable mention in Datlow and Windling's Year's Best Fantasy and Horror *in the year it was published.*

A complete surprise to me as I thought it poorly written. I've left this version mostly how it was originally published. This story also continues the theme of what is real and what is not—and how easily our perceptions can be altered. There is definitely a bastard product in this story, too.

WWPRO

The lights dimmed and the crowd whispered into silence. The chief judge coughed.

'The nominees for outstanding fantasy works published this calendar year are: Hugh Rookwell, for *Of Moonlit Dusk*, Wilson Crumber, for *Dragon's Flair*, and Mavis House, for *Goddess of the Conquering Dawn*.'

Applause punctuated each nomination. Wilson smiled when they called his name, and his wife Pam squeezed his hand.

'Ahem...' the judge began. She looked up and light reflected off her glasses. 'The winner is Hugh Rookwell for *Of Moonlit Dusk*.'

The world stopped. Wilson watched Hugh Rookwell head for the podium to accept the award for the second year running. His gut wrenched and he stifled a moan. He clapped woodenly in response to Hugh's acceptance speech, but couldn't shake the feeling of being left behind while the world sped ahead.

Pam tugged on his arm. 'I'm sorry, dear. I know you had your heart set on it. Next year, you'll see. You'll win then. Hugh's book was terrible good.'

'They'll never think I am good enough. *Dragon's Flair* is the best thing I have ever written. I don't think I can top it.'

Hugh walked past on his way back to his seat. With the award in one hand, he gripped Wilson on the shoulder and stood beside him.

'Coming to the post-award party, you two?'

Wilson opened his mouth to offer congratulations but the words got lost somewhere between his throat and tongue.

Pam said, 'Of course we'll be there. We're so happy for you, aren't we, Wil?'

'Yes…of course…very happy,' Wilson said.

'Come along, then,' Hugh said, and led them to the vestibule where drinks were already being served. A crowd was milling and voices caused a low rumble; camera flashes added to the storm.

Wilson grabbed a red wine from a passing waiter and Pam edged away to speak to a friend. He finished the wine and was admiring Pam's generous behind when he sensed someone close.

'You're one of the nominees, aren't you?' a young woman asked, a press badge crookedly attached to her lapel. She looked younger than his youngest child.

'Yes. Wilson Crumber.'

'Yes—Mr. Crumber. Can I ask you a few questions?' He nodded. 'What do you think are the most important skills for today's writer?'

'Well,' Wilson began as Pam rocked up with Hugh in tow. The young reporter's big brown eyes alighted on Hugh, forgetting Wilson.

'Mr. Rockwell. Congratulations. I was just discussing the necessary skills for a writer in this day and age with Mr.…uh…um.'

'Crumber,' Wilson interjected.

'Crumber. Do you have anything to add to our discussions?' Her eyes widened in response to Hugh's easy smile, quickly taking in his healthy tan and sharp, distinguished looks. Wilson couldn't help but add those to the list of Hugh's sins. Not only was he an award-winning novelist, he was single and very successful with the opposite sex. Wilson never saw him at the Writer's Centre without a different woman draped on his arm.

'In my opinion,' Hugh began, 'you must have a good understanding of grammar and syntax to write well. There must also be something of yourself invested in the characters. A well-crafted character can twist a plot and build the necessary tension to keep the story moving. Then, of course, you need a certain creative flair to really excel.'

The reporter scribbled down Hugh's words.

'Word processors help, but they can make you lazy. I don't agree with too much reliance on technology.' He tapped his head. 'It's the gray matter that counts.'

'Thank you so much, Mr. Rookwell,' the girl said. 'Would you mind posing for a photo?' She gestured to her cameraman, and Hugh posed for a few shots.

After the reporters moved away, Pam caught Wilson's elbow. He glanced into her still-youthful face and saw her blue eyes sparkle.

'Darling. Hugh's agreed to come to dinner next Thursday.'

Wilson's expression froze, then before he could blink, Hugh smiled and said, 'Nice of you to invite me, Wil. Perhaps we can talk about your work in progress.'

He hesitated, and Pam pinched him. 'Ow!...oh yes— glad to have you. I have a deadline, but I'm sure I can take time out.' He rubbed the spot where Pam had pinched him.

Hugh moved away, caught up in congratulations.

'We'd better leave now, Pam. The dog needs to be fed.'

'What?'

'Let's go,' he hissed into her ear.

'Oh pooh! You can be such a bore when you're in a sulk.'

'I'm not sulking—I'm depressed...there's a difference.'

'I'll drive then,' Pam said, making a grab for the keys. 'My nerves can't take your depressed driving.'

Wilson plonked himself in the front passenger seat and mechanically clipped in the seat belt.

'It is such a coup, getting Hugh to agree to come to dinner. Mel will be green with envy. She invited him last year and he declined. What do you think of that?'

Wilson sighed deeply and kept his eyes facing ahead.

'Wil...don't be a bore for god's sake! You didn't win, get over it. I mean, there is no use taking it out on me...God, I hate the silent treatment...Wilson?'

A few days later, after a bad breakfast, a lukewarm shower and sexual rejection, Wilson stumbled down the hall. He glanced into the hall mirror and rubbed the bridge of his nose where his spectacles usually sat. His eyes were red around the faded blue irises and his skin looked weathered. His bones ached.

Time, he thought. Not much time before age enfeebled him, before that frail collection of blood vessels and synaptic connections in his brain failed and his genius died.

A package addressed to him caught his attention. He tucked the parcel under his arm and headed for his study.

He had to work on his manuscript, but couldn't quite bring himself to turn his computer on. He slouched in his chair and let his gaze roam over the room before it settled on his mystery package. He frowned, then ripped off the masking tape and cardboard.

'Congratulations on your recent literary award nomination. As nominee for the All Australia Speculative Fiction Award we are happy to present you with WWPRO, our story-creation package developed specifically for writers. It contains in its knowledge base the collected works of all the world's great writers, from Nabokov, Chekhov, Hemingway, Austen and Hardy to modern-day writers such as Atwood, King and Clarke. These writers' works and biographies combine to provide an interpretive and interactive software package to help you produce your literary works faster and better than before. If you like our product and use it on a published work, all we ask is that you mention WWPRO in your book's acknowledgments.'

Included were installation guidelines and a further offer to trial a new, related product. His eyebrow gave a little shrug as he filled in the card. It was free and the software intrigued him. He leafed through the documentation. His mood lifted as he swung around to switch on his computer. While it was loading, he shifted a pile of reference books back to the bookshelf and made some space on his desk.

After installing the software, he spoke into the mouthpiece.

'A fox sat under the tree.'

The program interpreted and embellished.

The russet fur of the fox glowed darkly as it rested in the shade of a willow...

'Mmm... A trifle overdone, but not that bad.'

He spoke a very simple plot into the mouthpiece. After fifteen minutes he had a two-and–a-half–thousand-word story. Impressive. He turfed it out and continued to play with the options.

'Suggestion' mode displayed a list of synonyms.

In the 'assist' mode, the program quickly displayed comprehensive references where a phrase had been used before and included date and author. Reluctantly, he felt impressed.

He selected 'augment' mode, leaned back in his chair and dictated. He let his thoughts flow and he fantasized; he twisted his plot, he spoke sensuously, and he went on for hours. The program seemed to pick up on his tone of voice, the pauses, even sighs, as well as the words, and altered the prose accordingly.

Pam poked her head around the door. 'Wil,' she called, 'lunch is ready.' She disappeared and Wilson nearly toppled from his chair. He didn't stop to check the screen and went to eat.

She watched his face. 'I'm glad to see you're feeling better. I was beginning to get worried about you. I can always tell when you have writer's block.' She smiled.

He smiled back. His writer's block was gone.

After lunch, he returned to the study and checked his dictation. He had been so far into his own mind that he could hardly recollect what he had said.

'Whew... that's amazing. Did I really write all that?' he said.

He flicked through page after page on the screen. Every page had perfect punctuation, grammar and syntax. He pressed print and started reading the pages as they spewed out.

It was good. He couldn't believe how good. Somehow his mind and WWPRO had meshed and the result was stupendous and quick. Really quick.

Line after line flowed past his eyes. There seemed to be no need to edit and polish sentences. The words were his, the sentences; everything was in his distinctive style.

Ideas began rushing around his mind. After days of no inspiration he could barely sit still.

During the following days, he continued on. In the mornings he dictated and in the afternoons he read. No more endless polishing and editing. Words fell like feathers from his lips and floated leisurely onto the page.

Within the week he sent the completed manuscript to his agent.

Hugh arrived that evening for dinner. 'Congratulations!' Pam said, overriding his mumbled greetings.

'Thank you,' Hugh said, and grinned a huge grin. He looked suave as usual; his partner for the night the young reporter who'd interviewed him at the awards. He gave Pam a peck on the cheek and handed her a bottle of good red wine. After shaking Wilson's hand, he continued speaking. 'So, Wil. How's the work in progress?'

'It's finished—sent,' Wilson replied, unable to hide the grin of success in his voice.

'Yes,' Pam said. 'He's got this new-fangled software that helps him write. He's been in such a good mood since he got it.'

'Pam,' Wilson chided. 'That's not the reason I'm in a "good mood". It's just that my mind is working so well.'

'You're not talking about that WWPRO product, are you? Damn waste of time. I sent it right back,' Hugh said.

Wilson's jaw dropped. He closed it and replied, 'Yes...that's the one. Why would you send it back?'

'Because it's dangerous. Too much technology takes away the art from the craft. Call me old fashioned, but I can't abide them.'

Wilson scoffed and grabbed his glass of cabernet merlot.

Pam said, 'Don't you use a word processor, Hugh?'

'Yes, of course I do. But it's not the same as WWPRO. A word processor is much more passive than this new hyped-up thing.' He turned to Wilson and looked him straight in the eye. 'Don't use it, Wil. It will rot your brain.'

'You're overreacting, Hugh,' replied Wilson. 'It's just a tool.' At Hugh's look he quickly changed the topic, and the evening seemed to progress better from there.

He didn't sleep well, though. Hugh's words plagued him all night.

The next morning he looked at the WWPRO logo on the screen for an hour as he debated Hugh's warning against his own experience. Hugh was right, but when he looked at the logo again he rationalized that WWPRO had helped him reach inside himself and eased the creative flow.

With a sigh he set to work. He selected the option to maximize efficiency and artistic enhancement. He chose Chekov and Nabokov options with a twenty-five percent loading of Henry James. He had a momentary qualm about using it. Would it still be his work? He saved the options, casting doubt aside. He would show them. This time he would excel.

He couldn't wait to see the result.

Once again he entered his fantasy world and shifted his characters around like chess pieces. He embellished the forests of his landscapes, imagined the wildest creatures and visualized the slashing of golden blades stained with red blood. He floated free, godlike in the world of his making.

The next morning he read the previous night's work. He noted the slight Nabokov influences in the preciseness of his descriptions, a bitter sweetness in the underlying theme reminiscent of Chekov and realistic characterizations, with just a hint of Henry James. Of course, the dominant factor was his own creativity, his own style. It was the most exquisite piece of prose he had ever read, let alone written.

He reveled in WWPRO. It was a fantastic synthesis of his genius and machine.

Now he had time to spend with his wife. He no longer spent hours and hours glued to his computer. He had time to garden, to visit the neighbors. He even had time to visit his grandchildren.

The Monday post brought a second parcel. Wilson took it into his study and opened it hastily. It was another software package with additional hardware, an optional extra for WWPRO for a month's trial period. It consisted of a headpiece and a modem-like receiver to be hooked up to the computer.

Fascinated, he read on.

'Forget about voice activation, forget about sitting at your computer and compromising your posture. New, advanced WWPRO Extra works while you sleep. Yes, that's right. Just set up the thinking cap and sleep away. The very next morning you will have your most highly inspirational work prepared. Whether it be a thesis or a manuscript, just set the options and let WWPRO Extra do the rest.

'If you wish to purchase WWPRO Extra after the trial period, please send seven hundred and fifty dollars plus postage and handling to our sales department.

'*Caution: Do not use the product for prolonged periods or more than once a month.*'

Although the thought of having some machine hooked up to his mind made him cringe, he couldn't help being curious. What would unfiltered creatively read like? Would it combine truth and art?

In the battle between caution and curiosity, curiosity won.

That night he set up the machine and slept in his study. His dreams were vivid—wild horses stampeding, raging winds scouring the very reaches of his mind and ideas floating just out of reach.

He woke the next morning feeling sluggish. He ripped the headpiece off and dropped it on the desk.

The smell of coffee lured him into the kitchen and he guzzled the cupful his wife handed him. He gave Pam a hug, then dashed back into his study and looked at the printer. There it was: seven hundred pages of beautifully presented manuscript.

He spent the whole day reading it. The story was imaginative and epic. The language rich and liquid. And the characters! He almost wept at their inherent beauty. He had crafted a work beyond his own imaginings. This was what creativity looked like. This was where his true genius lay, deep in his mind, unfettered. It was not inhibited by the imperfect renderings of his conscious self.

He scribbled a check for WWPRO Extra and sent it off. He wanted to keep it.

The next day he had to try it again. Had to. Yet he felt afraid. He was tired. Not the work-all-night-at-the-computer tired, but something more. An empty tired. Hadn't he read a caution about not using the WWPRO Extra too much?

There was more to the story he had written, though. It was there inside his brain. It just needed WWPRO Extra to get it out. He found two aspirin and downed them. Just one more night shouldn't do any harm. He couldn't let Hugh beat him to the publisher. He had to get the timing right, otherwise he would be queued behind him for release dates.

That night he set up the equipment and slept in the study again, awaking the next day to the sound of his wife knocking on the door.

'Wil? Are you okay? It's nearly four in the afternoon,' Pam muttered through the locked door.

'Yes, I'm okay...I'll be out in a...in a...' he began, but faltered.

His mind was a blank. He couldn't find the right word to tell 'what's her name', the wife. He struggled up out of the chair and absently pulled the WWPRO Extra headpiece off.

He scraped his hand over his face. His beard was rough and he needed a shower. The last few days seemed to merge. Tired. Very tired, he thought.

He fell into a deep sleep, naked on the bed after his shower. The morning light punched through his haze when he next woke.

'What day is it?' he muttered. 'The manuscript!'

He rushed to his study to read his mind's outpourings. There it was, 1000 pages of perfectly typed and formatted manuscript.

He caressed it, kissed it and hugged it. He sat back and began to read. It was the masterpiece of his life.

'This time I'll get the Booker and the Hugo together,' he breathed. Sitting down at his computer, he began to type a note to his agent. He touched the 'K' and stared at it for a while. It seemed strange. He couldn't remember a 'K' looking like that. It took an hour to write the message to his agent.

After a dry three weeks where he'd barely dreamed or thought a single thought, Pam voiced her concerns. 'Why aren't you working in your study? Is everything all right?'

'Yes, dear...I'm fine,' he answered, and fell into a doze.

With the coming of a new month, Wilson felt the urge to try the WWPRO Extra again. The caution about using it returned to him. Once a month. Well, it was a new month.

The first two manuscripts sold within a week, and the publishers were begging to see synopses for his next books. The advances they offered were mind-boggling and there was already talk about awards.

He was going to reach that lifetime goal. He was going to be famous.

That night, he hooked up the headpiece and lay back on his couch. It was harder to fall to sleep than usual. He was cold. He could hear the modem whirring, and soon its monotonous tones lulled him to sleep. Pam woke him the next afternoon and helped him package up the new manuscript.

His movements were slow. His eyes drooped and his face sagged.

'You're always sad when you send manuscripts off, aren't you? Like they're your little children. Don't be glum,' Pam said.

Afterwards, he didn't talk much to his wife, as he was always too tired. He never had anything to say to the neighbors, the kids or the grandchildren, and they in turn grew used to the grunts of acknowledgment. He even stopped talking to himself. In fact, he never had anything to say, so he shrugged. He had vague recollections of truth and art, but they slipped away before he could grasp their meaning.

'...and the winner of the International Literary Excellence Award is Wilson Crumber.'

Pam screamed with delight and urged Wilson out of his seat. He stood and looked around, trying to remember where he was. He walked slowly to the podium. There were so many people, so much noise and confusion. A helping hand guided him to the microphone.

'Thank you...I am happy,' he began slowly. 'To...to...have award. My face is smiling.' He looked around, but couldn't recall what he was doing. He left the award on the podium and wandered off. He sauntered past the tanned handsome man whose name now escaped him.

'Wil—why did you walk past Hugh? He wanted to congratulate you,' Pam said. He didn't respond. Flustered, Pam herded him out of the ceremony.

As they drove off, Pam said, 'What in god's name is the matter with you?'

'Humph?' replied Wilson.

'I've never been so embarrassed. Wil? Are you sick? If you're not and this is a stunt, I don't think I want to speak to you again.'

'Humph.'

They returned home. A small packet was perched on the hall table; it was an upgrade for his WWPRO.

Wilson ambled off to his study. After fumbling with the packaging of the upgrade disk, he managed to insert it in the drive. While the upgrade was running, a promotion program displayed lists of all the new improvements. He sat down and stared. No words came. He couldn't spell. He couldn't think. He sat there for the rest of the day until Pam interrupted him with a cup of tea.

'Hello... darling?' his wife said. 'Hugh rang. He was very concerned about you.'

'Hmmph,' he replied, still watching the screen, the flash of color and form.

She placed a cup of tea next to his elbow. 'We never talk anymore, darling. You used to be so witty.'

Pam leaned against the back of his chair, 'Oh, look. You're listed as one of the famous authors.'

Hugh smiled, 'Hmmmm.'

When he said nothing else, she sighed, patted him on the shoulder and left.

Wilson sat and stared at the computer. After the promotion program ended, a new screen waited.

He tried to type. No words came. He couldn't spell. He couldn't think. He sat there for the rest of the day. He glanced out the window at the setting sun, and then back to the screen. He had managed to type, 'I kan spill katt.'

His eyes traveled to the head set. Perhaps it worked while you were awake. Reaching out, he slipped it over his head and heard the whir of the modem as it initiated.

Wilson stared at the computer and smiled. The screen remained blank. His smile faded as a cold emptiness filled his mind.

Another early story that featured a bastard product. I wish to thank Chris Andrews who edited Machinations *for all his hard work. This story is inspired by Roald Dahl and the admonishment about being careful what you wish for. As an aspiring writer at the time, I was keen to learn, keen to be good and I had a driving passion. I hadn't even been to an award ceremony or met many writers when I wrote this story.*

Verum Vivendi Sensus

It was a busy morning, the traffic was atrocious and it seemed as if every motorist Beth had come across was ten times more hurried than she was. She pulled up at a stoplight and noticed a red car behind her pull up close to her bumper. She looked up to her rear-vision mirror, as she was slightly angry that the driver had done that. It was the sort of thing that annoyed her on a busy morning while she was fighting the traffic. She could see the dark hair of the man and then she noticed movement—the lights had changed. She drove farther down the street. Still the car behind was persistently close. It bugged her and her anger started to seethe.

'The nerve of that guy,' she muttered over the sound of radio. She continued to drive and then the lights turned amber, then red. She pulled to a stop and caught a glimpse of the driver of the red car that had again abruptly stopped right behind her car. The light from the early morning sun slanted through the red car driver's window. Beth looked up to see who the maniac was that had started bugging her. When she looked, she froze: he had no face. All of his features were muted to the point that he did not have eyes, nose or mouth. The shock of what she saw made her lift her foot off the clutch and her car jerked forward and then stalled. Her head bumped on the windscreen and she exclaimed with an 'ouch' of pain. She shook her head and then heard the impatient toots; the lights had changed. She mechanically restarted the car and crossed the intersection. The man with no face turned off to the right.

She tried not to think about what she had just seen, tried very hard to remove it from her mind, because every time she replayed the scene she got gooseflesh and the sensation that someone had walked over her grave.

She parked her car and went to work. The day passed through the usual routine. As she drove home that evening, she pulled up at the lights near her home, where the shops were on the corner. She was just driving away when she saw a woman walking her dog, and that woman had no face. She was so startled that she didn't see the car in front stop and she barely avoided rear-ending it. Her car swerved to the left and the tires skidded. Horns tooted and people yelled, yet there was no damage. Beth tried, after she had righted the car, to catch sight of the woman, but she had turned down Leaf Street and was gone from sight.

As Beth watched television that night, the late news in fact, she yawned and did up an errant button on her pajamas. The newsreader read out the headlines and then the scene switched to an interview. The journalist was interviewing someone but their features were indistinct. Beth stood up to adjust the set. She played with the aerial and the picture was as clear as it was ever going to get. She made a cup of tea and threw out the remains of her dinner, then sat down again. Another story was screening and the faces were indistinct.

'Shit! What is wrong with the blasted TV?' she yelled to no one in particular. She persevered with the television and, as she casually watched the rest of the news, the obscure faces became blank and featureless. Then it dawned on her that they were just like the morning motorist and the evening lady walking the dog.

She quickly switched off the television and made some hot chocolate. Her hands shook with fear as she poured the hot milk into her mug, slopping white droplets on the bench and her hands. She shuffled up the hall in her lamb's wool slippers to bed. After climbing in, she leaned over and drank the hot chocolate, but her eyes were fixed and staring, still bearing the evidence of her shock. She numbly drank her warm drink and mechanically turned off the bedside lamp. However, she couldn't bring herself to slide under the covers or close her eyes.

In the morning, the cat's meow woke her and she quickly jumped out of bed to let it out. She had been asleep sitting up and her neck was sore. Her mind was a little fuddled and she couldn't remember much as she opened the door. The paperboy was passing by and waved. She waved back and did a double-take. She opened the door again and leaned out, her breath misting in the morning cold. The boy had moved away. She pulled her head back inside the doorway.

She tried to eat breakfast but for some reason she couldn't eat. Her neck hurt and she took some pain killers. She went to the phone and left a message at her work that she was sick and went back to bed.

She dozed fitfully until lunchtime and her dreams were strange. She dreamt she was at a large train station and it was jam-packed with people all crushing in on her. She looked around for a friendly face and the people she saw were faceless. She kept searching frantically and every single person she dared look in the face had no eyes, no nose and no mouth. She screamed and woke with a start.

'Damn pain killers do that to me every time,' she said to herself. She showered and then dressed in front of the mirror. She was getting on, she mused as she looked at her thickening middle and at the layer of persistent fat that wouldn't leave. She tied up her hair in a bun, and left the dyed-blonde bits hanging loose in a romantic fashion. She pulled on her jeans and looked around for a blouse to wear.

She left the house and went for a walk; her neck muscles were still tight, so she walked carefully, keeping her chin tucked in. She walked for half an hour and stopped occasionally to admire the autumn flowers and the pretty arrays of multicolored leaves. Walking past the primary school, she heard the children playing and kept going. She glanced idly over the fence and stood stock still. None of the children had any faces.

'God! This can't be happening!' She let out a strangled wail and a few of the children turned toward her and she saw their blank faces clearly. She backed up unthinkingly, shaking her head in disbelief. She heard an angry toot and jerked herself in the direction of the sound. A four-wheel-drive had pulled up next to her and she was standing in the middle of the road. She looked down and around, trying to take in the fact that she was in the middle of the road, and then she looked through the windscreen of the car. The driver had no face.

Her scream rent the air and she ran sightlessly across the street to head for home. People came out to see what the disturbance was and she looked around at them. They had no faces, too. She ran home, hiding her eyes from everyone. She kept her gaze to the pavement and found her way home. She fumbled for her keys, put them in the lock and swung the door open. She raced in as if pursued and slammed the door with her body. She stood leaning on the door, panting; her heart thundered in her breast.

She stumbled to her phone and rang her doctor's surgery. Luckily, she was able to get an appointment. The doorbell sounded not long after and Beth crept up to the door but didn't open it.

'Who is it?'

'It's me, Jocelyn from next door,' a shaky voice said.

'What do you want, Jocelyn? I'm not feeling well today.'

'Oh, I see. Well, I won't trouble you then. Perhaps I'll see you later.'

Beth started to cry, and a plaintive moan escaped her. Her neighbor went away and she sobbed into the oak of the front door.

৵৵৵

'Come in Beth. How can I help you today?' the doctor said. Then he noticed that Beth wouldn't look at him. She was hiding her head under her cardigan. He realized that she had been doing that in the waiting room, too.

'Beth? Look at me. What is it? I can't help you if you don't tell me what is bothering you,' he asked her again. At first she didn't reply, and then she spoke with her voice muffled from her cardigan. 'Doctor! I'm afraid I've gone crazy. You see...I'm sorry I can't tell you...it's really too bizarre.'

'Now, Beth, I have been your doctor for a long time and you know that I will look after you and that I would tell you straight if there was a problem. Tell me from the beginning.' He sat down in his chair and sipped his cup of tea.

Beth still kept her head covered as she brokenly told him of the faceless people that she had been seeing. First, the motorist then the others, until everybody didn't have a face.

The doctor sat and listened to her symptoms, occasionally murmuring an 'mmmm' of acknowledgment.

'Oh, Beth, you silly thing. I know exactly what condition you have and I have a treatment right here in my surgery.'

'What is it? What have I got?'

'You have what is called *Non verum vivendi sensus*, Latin for non-true sight. Now, if you lift up your head, I will put some drops in your eyes and everything will be fine again.'

Beth still kept her head under the cardigan and shivered visibly. 'I can't do it. I'm afraid you won't have a face and I...couldn't...bear it.'

'Okay. This is what we'll do. You close your eyes tight and take the cardigan off your head. Then I'll stand behind you. You won't see me. I want you to then look up to the ceiling and I'll put the drops in. After I have put the drops in, I need you to keep looking at the ceiling for five minutes. You will be fine. I guarantee it.'

A muffled 'yes' came from underneath the cardigan and slowly Beth lowered the garment and screwed her eyes shut. She lifted her head and opened her eyes to stare fixedly at the ceiling. She was trembling all over.

The doctor leaned over and placed two drops out of a brown bottle in both eyes. The drops stung and Beth had to struggle to keep from closing her eyes. Her trembling dislodged a droplet and it slid silently down her cheek and past her earlobe.

'Okay, Beth. You should be fine now. You can look at me. Don't be afraid.'

Beth took a deep breath that made her whole body shudder and then lowered her head. She kept her eyes closed and then she quickly opened them. Her doctor was smiling at her. He had blue eyes and grey eyebrows and his friendly, familiar smile creased his face. She let out a sigh of relief.

'Thank you, thank you so much. What caused it? Will it come back? I have never been so frightened in all my life.' She was breathing heavily, but otherwise she was relaxed.

'I am not sure what causes the eyesight to shift like that, Beth. The symptoms have been known to re-occur, so from now on you must have the drops put in every three months. Don't you worry now.' He leaned over and squeezed her shoulder as she stood to leave. 'There are no side-effects and you will see *Verum vivendi sensus* until the day you die.'

Another very early story, which I've left mostly as it was when it was published. The idea came from being tailgated and the way the sun slanted through to the car behind; it looked like the driver didn't have a face. Then I progressed that idea to: what if people really didn't have faces? Again, this story plays with perception—the idea that things are not what they appear on the surface and in this case some kind of group delusion.

Absence of Mind

The door flung open with a bang, bouncing on its hinges. Jo rushed out, catching her heel on the step, almost diving into the large pot plant by the door as she struggled to keep her balance. Righting herself, she fumbled through her handbag, searching for the car keys.

Her daughter Erin called out, 'Mum, what are you wearing?'

Jo looked down and sighed in the sharp morning light. She could see clearly that her blazer was navy blue.

'Oh shit!' she exclaimed and ripped off the jacket while stomping back inside the house to change. Her skirt was black and she hadn't noticed in the rush.

Finally, she made it back to the car and opened the boot. She leaned in to throw in her laptop and banged her head on the boot lid.

Cursing, she blamed her distraction on the big meeting occurring that morning. She rubbed her sore head and began going through all the details of the day while staring into space.

Erin called out again, 'Mum!'

But Jo didn't answer as she was still caught in the semi-chaotic thoughts that raced across her mind.

She didn't hear the crunch in the gravel behind her, and Erin yelled in her ear. 'Mum!'

Jo jerked upright, startled. 'Wwwhat?' she stammered as her head went up and impacted on the boot lid again. She groaned, holding her head, slightly stunned. 'For god's sake, don't sneak up on me like that. What do you want anyway?'

'You forgot about the excursion today. I need ten dollars.' Jo looked dumbfounded, trying to recall any conversation discussing money. In fact, she couldn't remember any conversation she had had with Erin or anybody else over the last few days. Rather than appear forgetful, she rummaged back through her purse, looking for her wallet. Grumbling under her breath that she really didn't have time for delays this morning.

The search through her bag was taking time; she checked it three times and at last admitted, 'I can't find my wallet!' She panicked. 'I don't know what's the matter with me.' She thought back, trying to recall the last time she'd seen it. She had used the credit card to buy some pizza the night before, and then she bought something on the internet.

She stomped back inside the house, her frustration increasing by the second. Her third pass through the computer room revealed her wallet by the computer, although she swore that it hadn't been there the last two times she looked. She handed over the cash to the eager grasp of her teenager and stormed out to the car.

Time was really becoming critical. She backed down the driveway, the engine screaming in protest.

Luckily, the power-walker who was about to cross her driveway knew Jo's modus operandi, hence he was able to hold his step in check. He did not want to join the mud splashes on her tires.

She successfully navigated the driveway and burned up the street. Speed was the last of her concerns as she was thinking of other things, until she came to the 'Give Way' sign and nearly collided with a rusty grey Holden.

The scent of a two-day-old hamburger made her nose itch and it commingled with the damp smell, which was the result of a slightly opened window when it had rained the night before. Idly, she thought about cleaning the car, when she had the time and when she could remember. She only noticed the dirt when she was in the car. At other times, its existence just floated away.

The radio blared loudly, playing a mixture of sixties and seventies music that Jo idly hummed to as she settled into the rhythm of the usual workday drive: turn left, a right, then through the roundabout, merging into the expressway feeder lane. Now singing loudly with her favorite 'golden oldie', she slowed when she saw that traffic was building up. She glanced at her watch; it was risky to get caught in the usual bottlenecks. She decided to take the turnoff and use the back road, which she used every other day. The traffic was beginning to clog up and she had to do some kamikaze driving to sneak into the turn-off lane, earning a few angry toots from the other impatients.

She relaxed at last, as the back way was scenic, routine and didn't require much attention. Soon she was mechanically driving along, her mind a million miles away. She changed down gear in preparation for the last turn, clicked on the indicator, turned and screeched to a halt. The tires skidded on the loose gravel and the front bumper stopped a hare's whisker away from the road barrier. The road had stopped.

Instantly alert, she looked around, not quite understanding her predicament. 'Damn! I must have taken a wrong turn.' She shivered. 'I really have to pay more attention, this is getting ridiculous.'

She reversed and doubled back, following the road she had driven down, going over in her mind the excuses she needed to come up with for the very important meeting that she was going to be embarrassingly late for.

She thought that it would be good to give work a call to let them know she would be late. She fumbled for the mobile phone as she drove. Driving one handed, blindly feeling around the tangled contents of her purse, she failed to find the shape of the phone. She sighed. The phone was still on the charger. She had forgotten to disconnect it. It wasn't a good day. She was never going to get to work.

She arrived back at the turnoff and saw the traffic up ahead vying for a place on the freeway. She pulled up at the intersection and checked the signs, looked around and was puzzled. It was the right turnoff. Perplexed, she couldn't think straight; maybe she had taken a wrong turn farther down. She did a U-turn and headed back down the road, deliberately paying attention to the roads she took. She took the first turn, then the second, passed over the bridge and smelt the polluted river as it lazily swilled the murk past its banks. *This is correct*, she thought, but she couldn't recall if she had passed it before. She had been on automatic then, so she just couldn't remember and that was that.

At the last turn she indicated, slowed and turned and slammed on the brakes. The brakes were rammed so hard that the car slid sideways, nearly sideswiping the barrier, which marked the end of the road. For some reason the road wasn't there anymore. Her mouth hung open and her mind went blank. 'I don't remember the road being closed. I must have made a wrong turn again.'

She slowly turned the car back the way she had come, determined again to follow the road back to the turnoff and logically follow the usual route to work. It had become a point of honor now to follow the road she wanted to take. She had decided not to battle the traffic and the bottlenecks. That's why she'd chosen this road. She wasn't about to back down now. This was by far the best route; there were no other cars and nobody around, just her and the road.

She backtracked again up the hill and over the bridge, past the brown stain of a river and around the curve. She slammed on the brakes again.

Another barrier blocked the road, identical to the other one. Surprised beyond words, she stepped out of the car, making sure to put the handbrake on. The sound of her feet crunching against the stones echoed in the country quiet. She stepped around the barrier, then knelt and examined it minutely. It wasn't new; the grey paint on the metal was pitted, peeled in places, and it was bent where something or someone had backed into it. Of where the road used to be, she could find no trace; it was an empty field populated with indifferent brown grass waving absently with the breeze. She closed her eyes, held them tight as the absence of the road sunk in.

In the distance, she heard the *woosh-woosh* as the cars sped past on the freeway, the sounds making her heartbeat match their rhythm. There was no evidence of the road she had traversed twice that morning. It wasn't there and she wasn't sure if there really had been a road. She really couldn't remember.

'Perhaps I took a wrong turn,' she said to the breeze and turned. A tendril of hair slipped from her haphazard bun, giving her a disheveled air. She walked limply back to the car, its red hue stinging her worn-out eyes. The radio still played its hackneyed tunes and she switched it off in irritation.

She started the car, revving heavily, and headed back down the road. She thought to take another road if she couldn't find the turnoff. If she couldn't turn, then she'd go straight. Straight was good. It went somewhere, after all. She went back over the bridge and down the hill and came to a dead end. There was a barrier in front of her and she looked to the side and there was the other one she had come across previously. *There were two of them!*

She stopped dead in the center of the road. It wasn't funny anymore. She sat and looked. To one side was the barrier that she had first found when she went to turn off. It was there, a meter or two off the main road. Now a meter or two in front was another barrier and she was certain that barrier hadn't been there before. She got out of the car, angrily slamming the door.

She stilled herself, tried to get calm and considered that she wasn't going to get anywhere if she decided to kick the living daylights out of the barrier. She strode over to the barrier, knelt down and looked at it. It wasn't new either. The bitumen stopped on the other side of the barrier in a neat cut and then there was the field again. She surveyed the spot, slowly turning her head; there was nothing there, no animals, or houses, just space. It smelt neutral and it was silent; only her breathing and the slight crunch of her shoes sounded in the quiet.

It was as if the road had never existed. Her heart beat painfully in her chest and her breath came in fast gasps. She slowly edged back toward the car, her eyes shifting from side to side. Her hand came into contact with the car and she turned quickly and jumped back in, feeling a desperate need to be out of there.

To hell with it, she thought, *I'll take the freeway.* She backed up straight, until she heard a loud crunch, a sprinkle of glass, and felt a jarring that heralded contact with a fixed object. Cursing and swearing, she got out to look at the mangled mash of her car and took in the barrier that she had crashed up against. Realizing that there was a barrier behind and in front and on the side: three of them. It didn't make sense at first; her mouth hung open. She was shocked, stunned, sure that she had lost all sense of direction or even her mind. It wasn't looking good. She ran around the other side of the car and yelped in surprise—there was a barrier there too. She walked around and around her car dazedly, unbelievingly.

She was parked on a section of crossroad, like a large crucifix marking the spot. There were no roads, no evidence of roads, only her, her red car and the bitumen beneath her feet. The grass waved indifferently, caressed by the breeze, barely acknowledging her presence. Her heart beat crazily as it rushed the blood through her veins, pounding loudly in her ears. A small whimper escaped her mouth.

She was alone.

The rest of the world had disappeared, lost in a moment of absence of mind.

This was my first published story and probably the first short story of length I wrote. I entered it in a competition that the Canberra Speculative Fiction Guild ran. It didn't win, but Geoffrey Maloney, who was one of the judges, talked about my story on the group's list. He encouraged me to polish it up and introduced me to one of the editors of Redsine, *Trent Jamieson. So it became my very first published story. I am so grateful for that encouragement and support and I've been writing ever since. This story idea arose from being stressed. Stressed all the time. Forgetting things. Always running here and there and not taking time. I used to take the back road to work and sometimes I'd be driving and I'd look around me and I wouldn't recognize where I was. I'd been driving in a dream. I would have to keep driving to work out where I was. It was scary sometimes. I wondered what would happen if I lost the world in a moment of absence of mind.*

In My Father's Footsteps

Night-stained clouds shrouded the sacred place as Binj followed Semyon toward it. The warder in white robes chanted, his words cut and sliced by lightning and thunder. Binj shivered and wiped his eyes, noticing how the rain glistened on Semyon's oil-slick body as his friend walked with head bowed. In many ways, Semyon's piety angered him. They had already trod their fathers' path, following their sires' journals to revisit sites traversed in their youths, and spoken with those their fathers once knew. Keepsakes and souvenirs accumulated by their fathers had been duly burnt and offered to their fathers' spirits.

Binj never wanted to take this step. Had promised not to.

Rain trickled down Binj's naked back as he knelt in front of the shrine's incense burner to waft scented smoke over himself. Gold and red embers teased out the bitter scent of myrrh and sent it curling upward, cleansing, mind-opening. He wished the scent chased away fear.

Fat raindrops smacked against the broad palm leaves that marked the entrance of the Home of the Ancestors. Bordered by swamp and hemmed in by foothills, it was a writhing, hungry jungle. None but the warders ventured there, unless one wished to walk the path.

Shadowed statues leaned over them, staring with cold, sculpted eyes that saw all and nothing. Lit by embers in smoke pots, a stone path stretched out ahead, leading the way to the fathers who, legend had it, dwelt on the edge of death.

The warder spoke. 'What do you seek, Semyon, son of Serun?'

'I seek to tread my father's path.'

The warder chanted another stanza to protect against the sins of the past, the sins of the fathers and the sins of the sons. 'Who travels with you to champion your soul?'

Binj raised his head. 'I, Binj, son of Lakti, will guard Semyon's soul.'

His proud face in showing no emotion, Semyon appeared oblivious to the storm that rocked the trees and tugged on the vines, his mind and soul focused on walking in the steps of his father.

The downpour eased to a consistent drizzle while they readied themselves. The air brewed, becoming like broth, hot and wet and fragrant. It was time.

The rhythmic hum of Semyon's prayer flowed over Binj in gentle waves. He waited until Semyon finished the final verse before moving to the base of the Great Father's statue to prepare the Wiyun root. In the flickering torch light, Semyon's tanned face looked calm. Binj knew his friend had always yearned to become closer to his father, who had died when he was a baby. Not knowing his father made walking the path so much more important to Semyon. In walking the path, it is said one could come to know one's ancestors intimately.

Binj took the knife from his loin cloth and scraped the skin of the Wiyun root. Then, as instructed by the warder, he cut it into thick slices, the purple juice dripping into his bowl. Using a pestle, he mashed the pieces into the wood of the bowl. His own father, Lakti, had used this same bowl when he trod his father's path. Yet Lakti had forbidden him to do the same, to tread in his steps. Binj had pondered this prohibition often but one did not question one's father. That would show disrespect, an unthinkable lack of faith. The ritual was sacred and secret, revealed only as the sons trod the path themselves.

When the juice rose above the grainy mass of fiber, Binj poured it into a cup. Once again Semyon chanted, rocking back and forth on his heels, preparing his mind for his journey. The name 'Serun' ended every stanza. Semyon's voice grew stronger, summoning his father's spirit to witness the journey. Bowing low, with hands raised above his head, Binj offered up the cup. Semyon took the bowl and sipped once, twice and then a third time. Binj drank off the dregs as befitted his station. His journey would echo Semyon's, but not eclipse it. His duty was to guide, to guard, and then return with his friend.

The Wiyun root was bitter on his tongue and left his throat numb. In no time at all, Binj's senses shifted and blurred. The light rain beat like a hundred drums and sour sweat dripped from his upper lip. The jungle groaned and swayed like a rabid dancer and the pathway was dark as an eager throat. Looming above him was Semyon, sweating as he clenched and unclenched his hands, with eyes fixed on the statue of the Great Father.

'Yes, father. I hear you. I will follow the path,' Semyon said, his voice flat.

Binj shifted his gaze to the old, weathered statue. The mouth appeared to move but Binj could hear nothing. All around him trees, leaves, and the stone path faded out of focus, then sharpened and then undulated. Binj's stomach twisted and he had to hold back the nausea lest he dishonor Semyon's quest. The darkness thickened, and the shifting light made the vine shadows dance and twirl. The smoke pots went out with a cough. The scent of incense mixed with the clean smell of palm leaves and the damp humus beneath. The full moon rose above the jungle, partially obscured by cloud. Its light made the stone path glow a ghostly grey, pockmarked with darker, diseased blotches. He wanted to turn away from it, from Semyon and his quest.

Just then, Semyon staggered. Binj leapt to steady him before he fell. Gaze unfocused, Semyon gestured down the narrow path and leaned on Binj. Binj bore his friend's weight and half-carried him along the path. Semyon's chant was now staccato, no longer a beautiful, flowing rhythm. It jarred.

The path rippled like a snake. Binj found it hard to walk in a straight line, having to steer the befuddled Semyon as well as negotiating a shifting path. Every time he put his foot down, the path moved under him. The rock rose to meet his bare foot then fell and twisted to the side. Lurching from step to step, Binj's heart rate quickened and he grunted, trying to keep hold of his burden.

The trees and vines wrestled together, struggling and worming around them. Could the Wiyun root affect him so much? What was Semyon seeing? His friend had consumed the bulk of the root. Ahead, man-sized shapes appeared and disappeared in the dark foliage. Binj had to shake his head. Was that a statue behind that large tree? Sweat obscured his vision. Shaking his head again, he peered into the dense jungle, the swirling mass of palm leaves and vines that shifted and turned. They kept to the roiling path, but there was no sign of anything else. What were they meant to do? There was nothing but path and the jungle.

Around a bend in the path, a stone statue thrust up through the ground. Binj looked down to find his feet were no longer on the path. Blades of grass poked up between his toes. He was alone. The air blurred and then he blinked. Nearby, Semyon knelt, his fingers brushing against the feet of the statue of a man. Trying to keep his eyes focused, Binj blinked and stared as Semyon rose up, kissed the stone face, and knelt again, head bowed in prayer.

The jungle leaned toward the small clearing, poised to erase it from existence. What should he do? Semyon appeared safe. Was that all there was to this ritual? Binj fought to clear his drugged haze, and then noticed another statue, one that drew him to it.

Leaving his friend, Binj walked slowly to the stone figure and had an immediate connection to it. It was like his father, but it was not his father. Perhaps it was a grandfather. Binj followed his friend's example and embraced and then kissed the stone image. The stone warmed at his touch. He drew in a surprised breath as his own skin began to cool.

Panicked, he jerked back, but there was some resistance. He tried again, a persistent pull. Finally, his hand came away clean. Examining it, he remembered that to walk in the father's footsteps you must give of yourself to your ancestors so they can walk the land again. He had not believed such a thing possible. Stepping back, he cast a glance over his shoulder. Semyon embraced the statue. Binj's eyes narrowed, reassessing. No, his friend was slumped over the stone image. Binj lurched to Semyon's aid.

The first tug achieved nothing. On closer examination he saw that Semyon's skin had adhered to the stone. He tried again and couldn't shift his friend. The drug pulled at his senses. Binj shook his head, but the Wiyun root's hold was still strong. He shouted in Semyon's ear. 'Let go. It is taking the life from you.'

Semyon heard him but was stuck fast. He moaned and rocked his head back and forward, trying to free himself. Binj gritted his teeth as he peeled Semyon's left hand off the stone. After placing Semyon's hand on his shoulder, Binj went for the right one. Semyon screamed as his skin separated from the surface of the statue. Binj pried off the rest of Semyon's naked body. Welts and bloodied grazes mottled the brown skin. Binj glanced over his shoulder at the statue, saw Semyon's blood disappear into the stone.

Binj thought of turning back. He swung around, dragging Semyon's semi-conscious body with him. The path no longer glowed in the moonlight. He blinked sweat from his eyes. The path faded from view.

He laid Semyon down. Beside the statue was a shallow offering bowl filled with rainwater. Taking off his loin cloth, he dipped the edge in the water and bathed Semyon's wounds. He now began his own chant, calling on his father for help. *Please father, give him strength. Forgive me, father, for I have disobeyed. I have walked in your steps.*

Semyon stirred. Eyes wild and unfocused, the chant came readily to his lips. Binj did not resist when Semyon fought his way to his hands and knees. Muscles flexed along his back as he crawled farther down the path, deeper into the jungle. Binj could not see his own ancestor's statue anymore. Over his shoulder, he saw Semyon's relative's image move, a hand opened then closed—one step closer to life. Binj tasted fear and wrapped his loincloth around his waist as he loped after Semyon.

Semyon mumbled while he crawled, mud clinging to his knees and his feet. The path swerved and curved as if alive. Binj's stomach writhed and he threw up. Stopping to wipe his mouth, he thought he heard voices, whispers among the shuffle and shifts of the foliage.

Images came then, slicing into his brain with sharp edges. A square room, hard surfaces, men talking, gesturing. There was something familiar about one of them. The words meant nothing. The language was long dead. The clothes, too, were from another time—the time before. He was walking in his father's footsteps, in his father's father's footsteps, seeing the world of the past. The image arrowed out of his mind to be replaced with another. This scene showed bodies piled high, bodies in ditches, bodies hanging from broken buildings. Faces frozen in fear.

Binj's pulse raced. These were things he did not wish to see. Denial did not help. He did not want the guilt, the first-hand account of past lives in his mind. Is this why his father had forbidden him the ritual?

If he was seeing this, what was Semyon experiencing? Semyon had had more of the Wiyun root, his will was more deeply entwined with the spirit of the quest. He actually wanted to walk the father's path. What would his forefathers' lives show him? Binj tried to shut his mind, to exclude the images. They wouldn't retract but stayed there like a weapon cleaving his skull. Binj had to keep moving.

'Semyon?' he called.

Binj found Semyon yelling at the top of his lungs. The words were meaningless but they sounded similar to the language in Binj's own visions. Semyon needed help to fight the recollections of the past. They were meant for glimpsing, not reliving. Perhaps the first encounter had weakened Semyon, making the visions more powerful.

'Semyon. Stop!'

With wide eyes, Semyon stared unseeingly. Nostrils flaring, arms twitching as if repelling unseen foes, the man fought for breath.

'Semyon, listen. These are visions from the past. You must fight them so we can meet your father. Serun must be farther along the path. We must go deeper.'

Semyon shuddered and his eyes gradually refocused. Binj shivered when he noted the fear in his friend's gaze and the haunted cast to his features. It reminded Binj of the dead he had seen in his own visions. Binj made Semyon lean on him and he half-carried him along the path. The effects of the Wiyun root were lessening. He was more in control, though fevered shivers shot up his legs and sweat cooled on his skin, despite the mugginess of the night air.

The next junction came into view. Here the statues were side-by-side. The image of his father, Lakti, was old, stooped and wrinkled, like the day he died. The statue of Semyon's father, Serun, showed a countenance and form captured in youth. A face that Binj didn't know, except in the resemblance to Semyon. A gasp wrenched from Semyon as he stumbled forward. Binj found himself mesmerized by his own father's statue. It looked so real. It called to him. Grief and loss swirled up, nearly choking him. He missed his father. Missed his wisdom and love.

A sharp cry, full of loss, drew him from his father's image. Semyon's weeping reached him, and he turned to watch as Semyon made his way to the foot of Serun's statue, at first touching the feet, then the lower edge of the carved robe.

Binj's gaze was caught by the expression in Serun's face, which was etched in a mask of loathing. A splinter of fear pierced his gut.

'No! Don't touch him!' But it was too late. Semyon collapsed at his father's feet, outstretched hands clasped around the statue's ankles.

Binj glanced toward his father, longing for the old man's counsel. Although he had disobeyed Lakti in walking the path, he thought his father would understand. His friend had wanted him to share this journey. How could he deny one he loved like a brother? All his life, his father had taught him to care for and nurture Semyon. His duty was to revere Semyon like an older brother. How could he have refused?

It was time for truth. He had to face his own father with his own misdeeds. With one last glance at Semyon, who shuddered and jerked as his life's energy was sucked from him, Binj climbed up the statue of his father so they could stand face to face. Closing his eyes, he leaned closer, touching nose to nose, forehead to forehead, thigh to thigh. Again the visions rushed into him, and then he detected the transfer of his life force, like a thin cord reeling in a fish. There was no panic with the sensation and no weakness. He trusted his father to let him live. His father's presence filled him up. Binj reveled in it, wanted to become lost in it—but Lakti pushed him away with a warning.

Binj leaped down and whirled, bringing his arms up to ward against the blow. It staggered him. Binj shook his head, realizing that Semyon was not Semyon, but Serun. His friend's face was riddled with hate. Another blow staggered Binj and forced him to his knees. Emotions whirled, some his own, most his father's.

This scene had played out before. How many times he did not know. Friends locked in a death battle, caught in hate that stretched back for generations. The awful truth shook Binj. Lakti had slain Serun, his dearest and closest friend. The grief was there, along with the bitter inevitability of fate. Binj tasted the remorse as the emotion washed over him, reliving the moment thirty years ago when his father had taken Serun's life.

Then the reason for his own social standing came bursting out of him. The best of everything—food, clothes and money—went to Semyon's family. Lakti had pledged himself to the son of his slain friend, bringing his family lower in status to expiate the crime, even though it was not of his own making. It was an age-old enmity, one that had a life of its own. Again a blow landed, fierce and strong. Semyon's breath thrust through clenched teeth and a corded neck. Binj steered the next blow to the side and circled around.

The path was gone. There was only this clearing, this battle. No other choice existed. Semyon held a branch and swung wildly and yelled, 'Death to you and yours. Death for my death.'

Lakti had a response and it crawled its frigid way to Binj's lips. 'This duel is not our own. The reasons for it are long dead. Stop, my friend.'

Another blow landed. Binj let it fall as his father had done. In the mud, he rolled, momentarily stunned. It was time to fight back. Reason would not win out. Binj grabbed his knife from underneath the folds of his loin cloth. He rose to his knees and used the statue of his father to assist him to stand. The presence of his father swelled inside him. The world went as black as the night around them. His arm swung, met flesh. Hot blood sprayed over his naked chest and began to congeal on his hands. The knife dropped into the mud. The rain came hard once again, battering him.

The spirit of Lakti could not let his son die, so it killed Semyon. Binj, his father's spirit already fled, found himself alone with the body. Staring at that once-loved face, he saw the features twisted with the hate of the father and wept. Why did it have to be like this?

Binj lurched out of the clearing, to tread the dull, stone path, now bathed in the mists of morning. Sunlight showed him the way out. Semyon's blood streaked his torso. He mourned for his friend and for what could have been.

The warders came swarming toward him. Somehow they knew the outcome. They bathed him, took away the blood but not the memory. They gave him back his clothes and let him walk the lonely path back to the village.

His wife waited for him on the veranda, their son in her lap. Her dark eyes held sorrow, even though she smiled in welcome relief. Her eyes looked beyond him and the smile died. Semyon did not follow triumphant. He followed on a bier. Binj walked past his wife and son toward Semyon's house. The cry of Semyon's baby son reached his ears. His friend's wife looked up, saw him, saw what followed. She didn't cry out but stood gravely.

The child squirmed in her arms as Binj made his pledge. He would support her and her child. The best of his crops would go to them. As he turned away, Semyon's wife wailed. Binj flinched and kept on walking.

As evening waned, he sat on the veranda and pondered what he would tell his son. His own father had forbidden him to walk in his footsteps. The truth of the ritual was hidden. Even now the details faded, wiped away as the last vestiges of the drugs left his system.

If Binj had been a good son, he would have listened to his father. He would have honored his wisdom. But he had been offered a choice and a test of his loyalty and he had made a mistake. His son, Leland, staggered over to him on wobbly legs. A tear fell down Binj's cheek. How could he stop this happening again? If they stayed, then Leland would be faced with the same choice. The ritual was a rite, a passage to manhood. If they stayed, no amount of warning would prevent it.

The only way to break this cycle was to take his footsteps out of their village. He had to be the one to break the circle.

Semyon's wife accepted the deeds to Binj's property and bowed low. His wife and son on the cart, Binj pulled them down the road. They were leaving for good. His son would have no footsteps to follow.

This story was inspired by studying my family history. I found that I was living quite close to where one of my great-great-grandfathers had lived. I wanted to walk in my ancestors' footsteps. I'm continually fascinated with what their lives must have been like and what they thought and felt. I am grateful to the wonderful Kaaron Warren for feedback on this story, which has not been published before.

Publication History

'Absence of Mind': *Redsine* magazine, Issue 6, editor Trent Jamieson, 2001

'Verum Vivendi Sensus': *Alternate Realities Ezine,* 2001

'The Doctor's Pill': *Redsine* magazine, Issue 10, editor Trent Jamieson, 2002

'WWPRO': *Machinations: an anthology of ingenious designs*, editor Chris Andrews, CSFG Publishing, 2002

'Veg Out': *Potato Monkey*, Issue 4, editor Ben Payne, 2006

'A Vagabond Rhyme': *Susurrus Magazine,* Evol 2, Issue 4, 2006

'Life Stealer': *Dead, Red Heart*, Ticonderoga Publications, editor Russell B. Farr, 2011

'Through These Eyes I See': *Mythic Resonance*, Specusphere, editor Stephen Thompson, 2012

'She'll Be Right': *Never Never Land*, CSFG Publishing, 2015

About Donna Maree Hanson

Donna Maree Hanson is a traditionally and independently published author of fantasy, science fiction and horror. She also writes paranormal romance under the pseudonym of Dani Kristoff. Her dark fantasy series (which some reviewers have called 'grim dark'), Dragon Wine, was published by Momentum Books (Pan Macmillan digital imprint) in 2014. *Shatterwing*: Part One, and *Skywatcher*: Part Two, are now re-published independently in digital and print-on-demand formats. *Deathwings* and *Bloodstorm* were published in 2017. The final installments in the Dragon Wine series are *Skyfire* and *Moonfall*, to be published in 2018.

In April 2015, Donna was awarded the A. Bertram Chandler Award for 'Outstanding Achievement in Australian Science Fiction' for her work in running science fiction conventions, publishing and broader SF community contribution. Donna also writes science fiction romance, with *Rayessa and the Space Pirates* and *Rae and Essa's Space Adventures* out with Escape Publishing. *Opi Battles the Space Pirates* was published independently in 2017. In 2016, Donna commenced her PhD candidature at the University of Canberra researching feminism in popular romance. Also available is her epic fantasy series the Silverlands: *Argenterra*, *Oathbound* and *Ungiven Land*.

In 2017, *Beneath the Floating City*, a collection of science fiction short stories by Donna, was shortlisted for an Australian Aurealis Award for best collection. In 2018, Donna published *Through These Eyes: Tales of magic realism and fantasy*. Donna lives in Canberra with her partner and fellow writer Matthew Farrer.

You can contact Donna at her
blog http://donnamareehanson.com

Or sign up to her newsletter, *Wing Dust*

Or on Twitter @DonnaMHanson
and www.facebook.com/donnamareehanson

Also by Donna Maree Hanson

The Silverlands (Epic Fantasy)

Argenterra: The Silverlands: Book One

Oathbound: The Silverlands: Book Two

Ungiven Land: The Silverlands: Book Three

Dragon Wine Series (Dark Fantasy)

Shatterwing: Dragon Wine: Part One

Skywatcher: Dragon Wine: Part Two

Deathwings: Dragon Wine: Part Three

Bloodstorm: Dragon Wine: Part Four

Skyfire: Dragon Wine: Part Five

Moonfall: Dragon Wine: Part Six

Love and Space Pirates (Science Fiction Romance)

Rayessa and the Space Pirates

Rae and Essa's Space Adventures

Opi Battles the Space Pirates

Short story collections

Beneath the Floating City, science fiction short stories